Praise for Lexi B........ ....ana Mercenaries...

"I can always trust Lexi Blake's Dominants to leave me breathless...and in love. If you want sensual, exciting BDSM wrapped in an awesome love story, then look for a Lexi Blake book."

~Cherise Sinclair USA Today Bestselling author

"Lexi Blake's MASTERS AND MERCENARIES series is beautifully written and deliciously hot. She's got a real way with both action and sex. I also love the way Blake writes her gorgeous Dom heroes--they make me want to do bad, bad things. Her heroines are intelligent and gutsy ladies whose taste for submission definitely does not make them dish rags. Can't wait for the next book!"

~Angela Knight, New York Times Bestselling author

"A Dom is Forever is action packed, both in the bedroom and out. Expect agents, spies, guns, killing and lots of kink as Liam goes after the mysterious Mr. Black and finds his past and his future... The action and espionage keep this story moving along quickly while the sex and kink provides a totally different type of interest. Everything is very well balanced and flows together wonderfully."

~A Night Owl "Top Pick", Terri, Night Owl Erotica

"A Dom Is Forever is everything that is good in erotic romance. The story was fast-paced and suspenseful, the characters were flawed but made me root for them every step of the way, and the hotness factor was off the charts mostly due to a bad boy Dom with a penchant for dirty talk."

~Rho, The Romance Reviews

"A good read that kept me on my toes, guessing until the big reveal, and thinking survival skills should be a must for all men."

~Chris, Night Owl Reviews

At Your Service

Other Books by Lexi Blake

ROMANTIC SUSPENSE

Masters and Mercenaries
The Dom Who Loved Me
The Men With The Golden Cuffs
A Dom is Forever
On Her Master's Secret Service
Sanctum: A Masters and Mercenaries Novella
Love and Let Die
Unconditional: A Masters and Mercenaries Novella
Dungeon Royale
Dungeon Games: A Masters and Mercenaries Novella
A View to a Thrill
Cherished: A Masters and Mercenaries Novella
You Only Love Twice
Luscious: Masters and Mercenaries~Topped
Adored: A Masters and Mercenaries Novella
Master No
Just One Taste: Masters and Mercenaries~Topped 2
From Sanctum with Love
Devoted: A Masters and Mercenaries Novella
Dominance Never Dies
Submission is Not Enough
Master Bits and Mercenary Bites~The Secret Recipes of Topped
Perfectly Paired: Masters and Mercenaries~Topped 3
For His Eyes Only
Arranged: A Masters and Mercenaries Novella
Love Another Day
At Your Service: Masters and Mercenaries~Topped 4
Master Bits and Mercenary Bites~Girls Night
Nobody Does It Better
Close Cover
Protected: A Masters and Mercenaries Novella
Enchanted: A Masters and Mercenaries Novella
Charmed: A Masters and Mercenaries Novella
Treasured: A Masters and Mercenaries Novella, Coming June 29, 2021

Masters and Mercenaries: The Forgotten
Lost Hearts (Memento Mori)

Lost and Found
Lost in You
Long Lost
No Love Lost

Masters and Mercenaries: Reloaded
Submission Impossible, Coming February 16, 2021

Butterfly Bayou
Butterfly Bayou
Bayou Baby
Bayou Dreaming
Bayou Beauty, Coming July 27, 2021

Lawless
Ruthless
Satisfaction
Revenge

Courting Justice
Order of Protection
Evidence of Desire

Masters Of Ménage (by Shayla Black and Lexi Blake)
Their Virgin Captive
Their Virgin's Secret
Their Virgin Concubine
Their Virgin Princess
Their Virgin Hostage
Their Virgin Secretary
Their Virgin Mistress

The Perfect Gentlemen (by Shayla Black and Lexi Blake)
Scandal Never Sleeps
Seduction in Session
Big Easy Temptation
Smoke and Sin
At the Pleasure of the President

URBAN FANTASY

Thieves
Steal the Light
Steal the Day
Steal the Moon
Steal the Sun
Steal the Night
Ripper
Addict
Sleeper
Outcast
Stealing Summer

LEXI BLAKE WRITING AS SOPHIE OAK

Texas Sirens
Small Town Siren
Siren in the City
Siren Enslaved
Siren Beloved
Siren in Waiting
Siren in Bloom
Siren Unleashed
Siren Reborn

Nights in Bliss, Colorado
Three to Ride
Two to Love
One to Keep
Lost in Bliss
Found in Bliss
Pure Bliss
Chasing Bliss
Once Upon a Time in Bliss
Back in Bliss
Sirens in Bliss
Happily Ever After in Bliss
Far From Bliss, Coming 2021

A Faery Story
Bound
Beast
Beauty

Standalone
Away From Me
Snowed In

At Your Service

Masters and Mercenaries: Topped
Book 4

Lexi Blake

At Your Service
Masters and Mercenaries~Topped Book 4

Published by DLZ Entertainment LLC at Smashwords

Copyright 2017 DLZ Entertainment LLC
Edited by Chloe Vale
ISBN: 978-1-937608-65-1

McKay-Taggart logo design by Charity Hendry

Lyrics from "Don't Call Me Darlin'" copyright Corinne Michaels, to appear in *Say You Won't Let Go*.

Acknowledgments

Thanks to the usual suspects: Kim Guidroz, Liz Berry, Kori Smith, Sara Buell, Riane Holt, Stormy Pate, Danielle Sanchez, Jillian Stein, Richard Blake, and Dylan Blake.

Special thanks to Corinne Michaels and Larissa Ione for letting me spend time with your characters as we build toward our crossover event! Meshing worlds is easy and amazing when you work with authors as talented as the two of you!

Sign up for Lexi Blake's newsletter
and be entered to win a $25 gift certificate
to the bookseller of your choice.

Join us for news, fun, and exclusive content
including free short stories.

There's a new contest every month!

Go to www.LexiBlake.net to subscribe.

Prologue

Javier winked at the gorgeous blonde as he fumbled with the keys to his apartment. Normally he didn't bring women back here. It was way easier to go to their place and sneak out after the sex was done, thus sparing them both an awkward morning, but Kristy was different.

At least he thought she might be.

They'd been seeing each other for a month. He'd met her at a private play party. She'd been there with a couple of friends, but she'd seemed drawn straight to him after the first hour. She'd shyly asked if they could play, and they'd been partners from then on. After a few raucous sessions, they'd decided to take their relationship into the vanilla world and see where they could go.

He'd taken her out with some friends tonight. If things went well, he might ask if he could bring her with him to Sanctum. Of course, she'd have to go through a bunch of checks and interviews because Sanctum was a private BDSM club. It would be good to have a sub at his side.

"Oh, Sir," she said, rubbing her body against his as though she couldn't even wait until they were inside. "I'm going to rock your world tonight."

After tonight, she wouldn't call him Sir again. It was time. He wasn't a child anymore and he was tired of one-night stands, had been for a while. He wasn't sure Kristy was the one, but he was willing to give it a go, and that started by inviting her to spend the night with him.

Letting her know where he lived. Had he really thought that? Maybe he was as bad as everyone said he was.

He slid the key in the door just as he caught sight of the new girl walking down the hall.

What was her name again? Julie? Juliana?

Jules. Chef had introduced her as Jules. She was the new hostess and she'd rented the apartment across from his. She was carrying an armful of groceries. Normally he would have helped her with that, but he had a horny blonde to deal with. A horny blonde whose hand was currently trying to run down his slacks.

She could be awfully aggressive when she wanted something. He tried to gently tug her hand up. This was a coworker and he was trying to rebrand himself as anything but a manwhore. Making out in the hallway was not going to help his reputation.

He managed to nod Jules's way. "Sorry. Uhm, it's been a night, you know."

Jules strode by them. "I don't think your night's over, buddy."

"It's definitely not," Kristy whispered far too loudly. "Not over at all." Kristy stopped, her body stiffening behind him. "Eww, what's wrong with her arm?"

Shit. He should have cut Kristy off at the fourth round of shots. They'd gone out with some of his friends from the club and it had been obvious that his Dom friends hadn't thought he'd been careful enough. Kristy had been a little loud, a bit too much. Now he agreed with them.

She hadn't behaved this way in the dungeon. She'd been practically perfect.

Jules turned, holding up her left arm. It had been amputated just below the elbow. He hadn't seen her without the prosthetic before. "I like to call her stumpy. What? You never seen a stump before? Don't knock it 'til you've tried it, sister."

"Hey," he called out, wanting to apologize.

"Don't worry about it." Jules managed to get her door open. "I don't care what a drunk fool thinks anyway."

And he'd made a friend. Her door slammed closed.

"She's weird." Kristy went back to wrapping herself around him.

"She's a coworker and you just embarrassed me." He opened the door and managed to unwind her, turning to look into her eyes. She was gorgeous, with wheat-colored hair and a body made to bang, but he really looked at her this time. She was a lovely woman, but there was a cruel twist to her lips and a hardness in her eyes he hadn't noticed before. "Do you understand that woman gave a part of her body to ensure that you can go out on a Friday night and drink too much tequila? She lost that arm during her service to our country. I could have done the same, but I was lucky."

She frowned, her bottom lip out in what he was sure she thought was a sexy pout. "What's up with you tonight? I thought we were having fun."

Maybe this wasn't going to work out the way he thought it was. "Come on. Let's go inside."

They might need to talk because if she was that rude to a woman she didn't know, how the hell was she going to handle his family? He had a brother in a wheelchair. Would she make fun of him, too? No. Optimism. He was going to be optimistic. She was drunk and in the morning, he would talk to her and have her apologize to Jules. There was no reason to ruin the whole night. It would be an object lesson.

But maybe he would keep the collar he'd purchased for her in his pocket. He might need a little more time to make that decision.

She was always sweet as pie around him. It was just the liquor.

Life was easier when his hookups happened in broom closets. He never had to see past how hot a chick was.

He closed the door behind him.

Kristy immediately turned and started to play with the buttons on her shirt. "Don't be mad at me. I can't stand the thought."

17

She was incredibly sexy. Curves in all the right places, and they were all artfully on display.

So why was he thinking about Jules and wishing he could walk to her apartment and apologize again? He didn't really know the woman, had only worked a few shifts with her, but he'd hated the blank look on her face. Oh, he'd heard her sarcastic words, but they'd covered up what had to have been at least a pain she'd become numb to.

Like his brother.

Kristy stepped in, turning her face up. "I can make it up to you, Sir."

What the hell was wrong with him? He was alone with a woman who was willing to have sex with him and he found himself thinking more about sleep than an orgasm. "I think it's late. Maybe we should go to bed and talk some more in the morning."

He should know more about her than her bra size and which lube she liked.

Her eyes had gone wide. "You want to go to sleep? It's not that late, Sir. I was rude. I'm sorry. What's my punishment? I think a spanking and then I should totally take care of you. I can make it all right and then maybe the next time we play, you'll take me to Sanctum."

He stopped. "What do you know about Sanctum?"

He'd never mentioned the club to her. It was a private space. He hadn't intended to mention it to her at all until he had cleared it through the owners.

Her eyes went wide. "Oh, some of the other subs I'm friends with were talking about it. They know that you and Eric and Deena are members there."

Eric and Deena were some of the friends he'd introduced her to. Eric had been his boss for a long time, teaching him much of what he knew. When Eric had left Top Dallas to be the executive chef at Top Fort Worth, he'd started having some play nights out in his neck of the woods. It wasn't the same as Sanctum, but he missed Eric and made time to go out to Fort Worth. After Eric met her, he'd told Javier to be cautious about Kristy, but then Eric kind of had it all so it was easy for him.

He was getting tired of being the manwhore. He was thirty and he had his dream job. It was time to settle down. Time to be serious, and he could be serious about a banging blonde babe who liked D/s.

And apparently knew about his connections to the most exclusive club in the state.

She looked up at him, giving him big doe eyes that might have worked on him before she'd mentioned Sanctum. "Come here, Sir. I think I should get you out of those clothes."

There was a hard knock on his door that startled Javi.

It was nearly midnight. Who the hell would be here?

Except any of a dozen women who could have tracked him down.

"Javier?" A female voice yelled through the door. "I know you're in there. Open up."

Kristy suddenly didn't look as sexy as she had the moment before. Or quite as drunk as she'd seemed. Her eyes had narrowed. "Who the hell is that? You have some other sub? Is she the one you take to Sanctum? I'm just some cheap piece of ass on the side."

Javier moved to the door. He recognized that angry female voice, though it wasn't usually directed at him. She was the one female he couldn't hide from. "It's my sister-in-law." He opened the door and stopped, his heart suddenly in his throat. "What happened?"

Sonja was standing there, his niece on her hip. Camilla was barely a year old and she clung to her mother, her eyes red rimmed with tears. Camilla was wearing a pair of brightly colored footie pajamas. Sonja looked worse for the wear. His sister-in-law always took care with her appearance. He'd never once seen her with her hair in disarray, mascara smudged. It looked like she'd managed to push his brother's wheelchair while she carried her child.

"What do you think happened, Javi? What happens every single night since he came home?" Sonja asked, sounding infinitely tired.

Rafe. His older brother. Rafe was in his wheelchair, slumped over as though he'd passed out, and he probably had. He was thinner than Javier had ever remembered seeing him, his hair greasy and unkempt.

19

Rafe stirred, his head coming up. "Bitch won't let me sleep."

Anger welled in Javi, warring with the guilt and shame he felt whenever he looked at his brother. Whenever he realized that it could have been him in that wheelchair having lost both legs in a helicopter crash. All it would have taken was a change of assignment, some bad luck.

There were days when Javier wished like hell it *had* been him. He didn't have a wife and child to take care of. No one would have cared if he'd devolved into some pathetic thing.

"I can't do it anymore." Sonja backed up, tears streaming down her face. "I took him in because he lost his last apartment and he was going to be homeless. He promised me he would try, but it's exactly like it was before the divorce. I hide the liquor and he has a buddy bring more over. He won't go to rehab. I set everything up for him but he cancels it the minute I go to work. He won't even try. He gets drunk and he scares the baby. I can't, Javi."

Javi's heart twisted. What was she saying? "Sonja, he's going to get better. He's got another surgery soon. He's going to get better."

"Fuck it," Rafe slurred. "Not doing the fucking surgery. Don't need you or her. Don't need anyone. Get the fuck out, Sonja."

Camilla started to cry, burying her face in her mother's neck.

"I have to think of my daughter," Sonja said, tears rolling down her face.

Javier remembered Sonja on her wedding day five years before. She'd been gloriously happy with her husband. Sonja had worn a white wedding dress and Rafe had been in his dress whites. Javier had stared at them as they'd danced and wondered if he'd ever find anyone who looked at him the way Sonja looked at Rafael.

How the hell had it all fallen apart?

His sister-in-law turned and walked down the hall toward the elevator, cradling her baby to her chest. Javier watched as Camilla's head came up, and she looked at her father as her mother swept her away.

And he was left with his brother.

"Do you need help getting him inside?"

He turned and realized the new girl was standing in the hallway. He hadn't noticed when she'd opened her door and stepped outside.

Rafe. He had to get Rafe inside. The neighbors were opening their doors and watching the scene playing out in the hall with curious eyes. Shit. If he didn't hurry, someone would call the cops and he would have that headache to deal with.

"I can get him in," he stuttered as he moved around, getting behind the chair.

"Who is that?" Kristy stared at his brother like he was a bug she needed some man in her life to sweep away so it didn't disturb her.

"He's my brother," he said under his breath, well aware lots of people were listening in. He pushed the chair forward but it didn't go anywhere. He tried again. What was wrong with the chair? Damn it. He didn't know how to work it. Rafe wouldn't let him near the chair. It was a serious point of contention since his brother had come home.

"He can't stay here," Kristy insisted. "I thought we were going to have fun. I'm not some nursemaid. He should be in a hospital or something. He looks sick."

"He's my brother." His head was racing. He needed to get inside. Why wasn't the chair moving?

"The brakes are on," a calm voice said. "Let me help you. Hold the door open for me and we'll get him inside and away from prying eyes. You would think they'd never seen a dude in a wheelchair."

The new girl was standing there, her soothing voice reaching out to him. He moved out of her way and she competently flipped the brakes off and pulled the chair back, though she only had one hand.

"I've certainly seen men in wheelchairs," Mrs. Gleeson from 5E said, holding her robe closed. "I'm eighty-two. It's how all the men I date get around. You work that chair well, dear. You're not Javier's usual. Much more lovely."

Kristy stepped out, frowning. "She's not his girlfriend."

Mrs. Gleeson sighed as she looked her over. "Yes, that's what I was expecting. Oh, well. If the gentleman in the wheelchair needs a hangover cure in the morning, come down. I've got a wonderful herbal tonic. I'm going to dip into the wine this evening."

"Could you keep it down?" Mr. Cassidy from 5F shifted his glasses and frowned.

Mrs. Gleeson shook her head. "Oh, go back to bed, old man. Have you never seen a man in a wheelchair, his brother who has terrible taste in women, a blonde tart, and a lovely female veteran who's trying to help out?" She waved down the hallway toward Jules. "Let me know if you're single, dear. I have two grandsons."

Javier felt his face flame as Rafe's head came up.

"Where the fuck am I?" Rafe nearly shouted.

"Go back to sleep, buddy. It's definitely time to sleep it off," Jules said quietly.

"Don't go. Sonja, baby, I didn't mean it," he mumbled. His eyes were completely unfocused.

How deep had Rafe fallen?

"It's okay. No one's going anywhere. Go to sleep," she replied, not missing a beat. "We can talk in the morning."

She pushed the wheelchair, easing it inside the apartment.

Kristy was hard on her heels. "Who the fuck is she and why is that man here? Javier, I'm patient, but this is too much."

Jules looked over at her. "Then you should go because apparently this is his brother and he needs help. Are you going to help? Or are you going to whine and cause more problems for your boyfriend here? Javier needs someone who can help him get these prosthetics off and get his brother into bed. I am more than willing to turn that job over to his loving girlfriend, but you look way more like a chick who runs at the first given opportunity. Which one is it going to be?"

Kristy stared at her like she wasn't sure what to say.

Javier knew. "I think you should leave, Kristy. I'll call you a cab."

She turned on him. "Don't bother. You're not the man I thought you were. I thought a Dom from Sanctum wouldn't live in a hellhole. It's not worth it. I'll find another way."

She stalked out the door, slamming it behind her.

"Well, I showed her, didn't I?" It wasn't really a hellhole. Of course, it wasn't all that nice either.

Jules glanced back at him, her lips quirking up. "Sanctum? Is that the club Chef and Mrs. Taggart mentioned? I bet it's full of rich dudes."

"Not all of us are rich. Some of us just work for the rich dudes." So much for settling down.

Except apparently now he had a brother to take care of. An alcoholic double amputee with a terrible attitude.

"It's better to know now. Sorry, I heard a rumor she's a new girlfriend, not a long-time thing," Jules commented.

Ah, the rumor mill was still strong at Top. "Yeah, it wasn't anything serious. Thanks for helping."

Jules put the brakes on again. "No problem. Do you know how to get his prosthetics off? He should sleep without them. He'll be more comfortable."

How had she known? He shook his head because his brother was wearing cutoff sweats and his legs were visible. Not something Rafe would have done had he known he was going out for the evening.

His brother had always been impeccable. But then this man wasn't really his brother since his brother would never, in a million years, call his wife a bitch and scare his tiny daughter. Ex-wife.

What the fuck was he going to do?

"Hey, one step at a time. I know this is overwhelming but the only way to handle it is to work the problem in front of you. Getting him to bed. Unless you want to call someone. Is there anyone else who'll take him?" Jules's logical questions and competent demeanor were something he could cling to.

He tried to shove aside the emotional storm playing through his brain. He shook his head. There was no one he could call. His mother lived in an assisted living facility. His father had passed years before. His sister had her own family to take care of and his younger brother had recently graduated high school and joined the Army, following in his and Rafe's footsteps.

"You could call the cops," she said gently, not a hint of judgment in her tone. "They could help you figure out where to take him."

"Of course not." They were just the words he needed to get him moving. She was right. He needed to work the problem in front of him and then get some sleep. There would be a world of new problems to solve tomorrow. He looked up at the woman who was showing him such kindness. "I'm sorry about what Kristy said to you earlier. She was never mean before. I guess I didn't really know her."

"You knew her bra size," Jules replied with a grin. "That's all most guys need to know about a woman like her. Hey, she was hot. I'm not so hetero I can't see that."

"Yep, she was hot. And then she wasn't. At least not for me." He had a suspicion now that her hots for him were all about getting into Sanctum, where she likely would have found a wealthier, more powerful Dom and left him behind.

Jules knelt down beside him and showed him how to pull his brother's C-legs off, how to clean and dry his stumps, how to ease him onto the bed without hurting him. Rafe was deadweight. If Jules struggled with her part, he didn't see it. She didn't complain or show strain.

She even seemed to know that he needed a minute. She walked out of his bedroom after they'd gotten Rafe into bed.

He stared at his brother, wondering what the hell he was going to do now.

Rafe had been his rock. Rafe had been the leader. He was only two years older, but it had always been Rafe who would go first into anything. It would all be easy if Rafe had been a shitty brother, but he'd never shut Javier out, never told him he couldn't go along because he was a snot-nosed kid brother.

Who the hell was he now?

Javier grabbed a blanket and a couple of pillows. He would bunk down on the couch until he figured out what to do.

He stepped back out into his living room and the redhead was there. She'd poured a couple of fingers of whiskey into a glass and held it out for him.

"You should enjoy this now. I think you probably need to get rid of it in the morning."

He took it from her. He definitely hadn't had enough to drink.

He'd been driving and planning to play, so he'd had exactly one beer hours before. He took the glass and downed a healthy portion.

"I've written down a couple of numbers for you." She gestured to a notepad on his bar. "One of them is a really good rehab place not far from here. I actually go there on a regular basis and they're super good at what they do. I left you the number for a…well, he's a guy who works with vets."

Javier could guess. "Kai Ferguson? Yeah, I think Rafe's already given up on that."

She shrugged. "Kai's a good guy to talk to anyway. I've only had a couple of sessions with him and he knows what he's doing. He could give you advice. The other number is a veteran service's group that will do everything from helping to set up doctor's appointments to getting him to and from rehab. They'll also probably send a nurse if he qualifies."

It was too much. He couldn't pivot and change that quickly. One minute he'd been dipping his toe into having a girlfriend who knew where he lived, and now he had a brother who would be dependent on him. And Rafe would be angry about it.

"Are you okay?" Jules asked.

"Why are you being nice to me?" He took another drink. If Rafe was staying, he would have to hide the liquor. Or do what she'd said and get rid of it because he was going to be responsible for his big brother, and it looked like the party was over.

She held up her left arm, showing off the stump it ended in. "I kind of know where he's been. I definitely know what it's like to feel alone."

"Well, I'm pretty sure Rafe wants to be alone." He couldn't get the look in his niece's eyes out of his head.

Jules moved to the door. "I was talking about you. If you need help with him in the morning, you know where I am. See you at work."

She closed the door behind her and he was alone again.

He sat up for the longest time knowing his whole world had changed.

Chapter One

One month later

Juliana O'Neil stared down at the petite brunette named Suzanne and wondered if she was a bored housewife. She had that look about her. Not the bored part, exactly. The woman had a glow, a certain innocent awe for the little things that made Jules wonder how often she got out. The housewife part she fit. She looked like the kind of woman who had a husband she would dote on and a couple of kids who adored her.

So what the hell had gone so wrong that Suzanne was here trolling?

It was the fact that sweet woman with the Southern accent couldn't seem to take her eyes off Javier that caught Jules's attention. Had she met the gorgeous chef somewhere, he did what he did with all women, and now she followed him around like a puppy?

Somehow the idea of Suzanne finding a broom closet and having fun with the handsome chef didn't sit right with Jules.

"Was everything all right with your dinner?" Jules wasn't sure how to go about trying to save a woman. Not that she hadn't before.

She'd totally saved people from mortar fire and bad guys. She'd been there, done that, gotten the T-shirt, which in this case was more like got the completely shitty prosthetic. Saving a woman from herself and picking the wrong dude to moon over was a completely new experience.

Suzanne glanced up from where she'd been staring and flashed a bright smile. "It was amazing. Truly. It was the best of all the meals I've had here. The bacon wrapped shrimp were better this evening. Not that they weren't excellent when I had them two days ago, but this evening there was something...some extra zing to them."

Suzanne waved a hand and Jules caught a glimpse of something on her inner wrist. Was that a brand? Maybe the sweet-looking housewife type had some secrets of her own.

"I tweaked the barbecue sauce they use. I didn't do it myself, obviously. I merely mentioned that adding some cayenne would boost the flavor," she admitted.

"I thought you were the hostess. I didn't realize you were a chef." Suzanne's face brightened. "That's very exciting. I love to cook. I would love to talk to you about the beef Wellington I had last night. The pastry was perfection. Do you make your own pastry dough or use a frozen puff pastry? I tried my hand with it, but it's surprisingly delicate."

Jules held up her obviously fake hand. "No, I'm not a chef. I simply help out in the kitchen from time to time. And I do believe the chefs make their own pastry. I wouldn't be able to."

Suzanne frowned. "Why not?"

Did she not see the prosthetic? "Cooking is one of those things that requires two hands for real precision. I only have one now and it's not even my dominant hand. I was a lefty and now it's gone. I'm not saying I can't heat a can of soup, but cooking is an art form."

"So is surviving," Suzanne said with a wistful smile. "I think you could probably do anything you would like, but sometimes dreams shift. You seem to know how to fix a recipe."

"Like I said, I help out." She'd been thinking a lot lately about doing more.

"How long have you been at Top?" Suzanne asked, her eyes straying back to the bar.

"I hired on six weeks ago." Yep, there it was, that longing look in her new friend's eyes. How to handle this? Jules caught Ally's stare across the room. Ally Miles was one of the servers, and she, along with Tiffany Lowe, had come up with the "save the civilian" plan. Ally nodded her way, encouraging her to continue. "I noticed you come in a lot."

Suzanne nodded, her eyes still on the bar where Javier was sitting with a couple of friends. "Yes, I was quite happy to find this place. I'm recently moved here. Starting a new job and a new life, so to speak. It's nice to find places where I feel comfortable."

What did she say now? She wasn't any good at this. Damn it. Why had she stopped at Suzanne's table? If she'd just gone on about her business it could be Ally over here awkwardly warning a perfect stranger about venereal diseases. This was Ally's table after all. It should be her job, but she'd found herself asking Suzanne about how the meal had gone. "I'm new myself. You know new girls gotta stick together."

"Oh, yes, we do," Suzanne agreed, leaning in. "Which is why I hope you'll allow me to give you some advice. I'm very good at seeing things like this."

"Things like this? What is *this*?"

Suzanne's eyes lit up. "Sparks between people. You see, some in my family think I'm a bit of a busybody, but I like to think of it as using all my gifts for the betterment of humanity."

"Gifts?" Was she losing control of the conversation? Now that she thought of it, she was kind of the one being a busybody. Who was she to care if some housewife went looking for a wild time with a bad boy?

Except Suzanne was sweet and Jules wasn't sure she was capable of not falling for whoever she slept with. Unlike her. Hell, she'd managed to marry a man she hadn't loved. She was fairly certain love wasn't real, but Suzanne would believe.

"I'm a bit of a matchmaker," Suzanne admitted, proving Jules right on everything she'd been thinking. "I mean I was way back in college. I might be a little rusty, but I think I've found your match."

Well, at least they were talking about dating. It would be a good opening to warn her gently away from the manwhore of Top. Over the couple of weeks she'd known the dude, she'd heard story after story about his sexual proclivities. "I recently got divorced. Well, I got divorced eighteen months ago. It was amicable, but I'm not ready to date."

There was no room in her life for a relationship. No way. No how. But would it be so bad to have a one-night stand? Every now and then.

Or a relationship based purely on need. Like some of the women who worked here had found at Sanctum. When she'd hired on, she'd gotten the spiel from Grace Taggart about the club many of the employees belonged to. They weren't taking new members for the time being, but when they opened it up again, Jules would have a place if she wanted it.

A place in a BDSM club.

Yeah, she wasn't sure about that, but she also wasn't willing to count it out.

"I think you can do anything you put your mind to, Juliana." Suzanne practically had a halo around her. She was sitting in exactly the right way to be illuminated by the soft light from the table behind her. "You just have to believe in yourself and the people around you. You can't let anything hold you back. Not when you want something. Not when it's right. I can practically feel the chemistry between you and that lovely man over at the bar."

"Linc?" Lincoln was the bartender. He was cool, though a little on the paranoid side. He was putting a beer in front of Declan Burke, one of the bodyguards who worked for McKay-Taggart. He was a lovely man, but he rarely talked. He seemed to prefer brooding and working out when he wasn't on duty. "Or Declan? Because I'm really not interested in improving my psych skills, if you know what I mean."

"They are not crazy," Suzanne said primly. "Though they might behave that way some of the time. I assure you their behavior seems perfectly normal to each of those men. You would do well to be more tolerant of the people around you. And no, I was talking about the other one. I think his name is Javier."

She bit back a laugh. Wasn't the world a crazy thing? "I was coming over to warn you away from him. That's funny."

Suzanne looked entirely satisfied with herself. "Then I was right. I've watched you two. I don't have anything better to do. My job hasn't started in earnest yet. I need a hobby. I think you should be the one to make the first move. He watches you, but he seems uncertain. Is he going through something? That might be why he's hesitating. I think all it would take is you asking him for a drink and he'll fall right into your arms."

"Arm," she corrected. "I'm not good with the prosthetic yet. I would probably drop him. I'm afraid you're wrong. The servers are worried about you and they wanted someone to kind of gently give you the truth about Javi. I wasn't going to warn you away because I want him for myself. I live across the hall from that guy and he's a serious player. I mean a walking, talking venereal disease according to the rumors. I've only been here for a while, but I know not to walk into the broom closet if I hear something weird."

At least that was what Ally had told her. She'd never actually caught Javier with his pants down, though she'd seen plenty of women doing the walk of shame out of his apartment during the first few weeks. It had been just after that night she'd helped him with his brother. She'd been surprised because he hadn't called her to help out again, and he seemed to have found a way to watch his brother while keeping up with his active social life.

And then the last two weeks he'd gone quiet and it made her wonder what was going on. No late-night dates. No early morning good-byes.

Suzanne shook her head. "You can't blame a man for his past. Can you honestly tell me you have no interest in him?"

"He's hot." She wouldn't lie about that. The man was sex on a stick, which was probably why all those women made the long trek down the hallway in the morning, still shaking in their stilettos. "I can't deny that. He's a beautiful man and he's pretty funny and nice, but I'm not interested in a relationship."

But then was he? He wasn't a serious guy. He was the very definition of good-time guy. She suspected he was taking out a whole lot of stress on those women he brought home. She had stress. Would it be wrong to take it out together?

Suzanne looked thoughtful for a moment. "I guess I was wrong. I've seen how you look at him, too."

"I don't look at him." Did she? "I mean I look at him, of course. I have to. I work with him, but I don't look-look at him."

One brow arched over Suzanne's eyes.

That was one judgmental brow. "Fine. I look at him but only because he's hot. I've got eyes. But I also know when something's bad for me."

"Have you had a relationship since you lost your hand?" Suzanne asked quietly.

This was the point when she would normally shut down all talk and walk away. She didn't have to answer this woman's incredibly invasive questions. They didn't know each other from Adam. She wasn't sure why she found herself holding the menus to her chest with her good arm as she replied. "No, but I'm okay with it. I'm not all self-conscious. I lost my hand. I would do it again because it saved some really nice people. If some dude can't handle it, I wouldn't want to be with him anyway."

"That's a good attitude to have, but do you honestly believe you've moved on? Juliana, you're working as a hostess for barely above minimum wage when your mother would pay you well to work for her."

A chill went up Jules's spine as so much about the woman in front of her fell into place. "My mother sent you."

Her mother. America's Favorite Hostess. Annaliese O'Neil was known across the country for her exquisite taste. She was a media queen with two television shows, a lifestyle website, and multiple cookbook and decorating book deals.

Yet, Jules remembered standing by the roadside with her trying to sell jam. She would make strawberry jam with her mom after Dad left them behind with nothing but a stack of bills. She remembered her mother crying and wringing her hands, and then standing up calmly to get to work because they had to make money and she only knew how to do one thing.

Jules also remembered the day her mother had told her not to call again, that she couldn't handle watching her daughter ruin her life.

"My mother made herself very clear when I left home to join the Navy. I wasn't welcome back."

Despite her chilly tone, Suzanne still seemed warm, her eyes sympathetic. "Sometimes people say things in the heat of the moment that they regret. She hasn't tried to contact you?"

Jules would give her mom credit. This chick was way better than sending some assistant around to get her to sign paperwork or to ensure she didn't talk to the reporter writing a tell-all story. Suzanne was slick. She'd spent days being sweet to everyone and getting under Jules's skin. "My mother contacts me when she needs something from me. That's all."

"I heard she paid for your divorce," Suzanne reminded her. "That was kind of her."

"She wanted to make sure Kevin didn't have any way to come after her fortune. That was her grand sympathy for me." Though she had sent her a card. That was her mom. Polite to the end. She'd likely gotten a blog post out of it—"Ten Ways to Support Your Daughter's Divorce." Probably would make a fortune off a whole new line of tastefully designed greeting cards.

"Or she wanted to make sure her daughter had what she needed," Suzanne replied. "Maybe it's not my place, but have you thought about the fact that she might have been reaching out?"

"It is absolutely not your place. Please tell my mother that if she wants to talk to me, she can pick up a phone." Not that Jules would answer, but it was time to walk away.

Suzanne reached out, putting a hand on her arm, right above the spot where the prosthetic attached. "Sometimes it only takes a little bend to save the whole tree. Regret and guilt can do terrible things to a person. The kinds of things only forgiveness can heal. Just think about what I said. And think about Javier. Remember that a pretty face can hide much pain."

Jules pulled away. "Maybe you shouldn't come here again."

Suzanne sat back, a sad smile on her face. "But then I would miss tomorrow's special. I don't know what it is, but I'm sure it will be amazing. I'll be here for a while, Juliana. If you need to talk, come and see me. And you should write down that barbecue sauce recipe. It was delicious. Sometimes circumstances change, but that doesn't mean you have to let go of your dreams. It merely means you adapt and come out of it stronger than before."

Jules turned and walked away, not wanting to talk anymore.

Dreams. She'd already walked away from those. She'd wanted something real, something that was hers, and the Navy had offered it to her. She'd needed to feel like life wasn't planned, like she wasn't merely slated to take over where her mother left off.

Well, she'd gotten that life.

She couldn't cook. Her dominant hand was gone and she was lucky to be able to hold menus in the one that was left. All she could do now was make a suggestion here or there and pray the chefs weren't douchebags who thought their food was far too perfect for a hostess to comment on.

Javier had been sweet when she'd suggested adding the cayenne. He hadn't looked offended at all. And he'd given her the credit when Chef Taggart had called him out for the sauce.

She glanced back to the dining room. Dinner service was over and there were only a few tables left finishing up. Javier smiled her way and held up his glass, as though offering her a toast.

Raven black hair. Chocolate-colored eyes. A jawline a superhero would be proud of. And that didn't even cover how stunningly perfect his body was.

She nodded his way and then walked back into the kitchen.

Would it be so bad to get in line? As long as she remembered exactly what he was, would it be wrong to enjoy a single night with him?

She needed to think and it was far easier to think about Javier than the problems with her mother.

Jules moved back to the office and started getting the menus ready for tomorrow. Pork tenderloin with pineapple was the special.

Savory and sweet. Just like she liked it.

She settled in and tried to forget about the ridiculously hot man in the bar.

* * * *

"What's up with the brunette? She's been in every night this week, and let me tell you, she can put away some food. She's tiny. I have no idea where it goes." Javier Leones shook his head and turned back to his beer. It was closing time and his station was immaculate. He could head home, but then he would have to deal with his brother and the fact that his world had imploded. Sitting here at the bar and having family dinner after work seemed like the better bet.

It was the tradition at Top. After the doors closed at ten and all the patrons were gone, anyone who wanted to was welcome to sit down and have a meal with all the leftovers. Sometimes it was leftovers. Sometimes it was experiments. It didn't matter because it was almost always delicious.

Except the time Chef decided to see what he could really do with tofu.

Linc glanced out over the bar as he wiped it down. He'd already pulled the wine for family dinner, and anyone who wanted a beer would have to get his or her own bottle. Otherwise, the bar was closed. "The weird one with the crazy eyes?"

"She doesn't have crazy eyes." Javier thought she looked kind of sweet. A little naïve. Like a sweet country mouse coming to the big city for the first time. "I think she's just impressed with stuff."

Declan Burke stared straight ahead. "I don't know who you guys are talking about. I haven't noticed anyone new. Not since Jules showed up. Jules doesn't have crazy eyes. She's got perfectly nice eyes."

The big bodyguard put a hand to his head.

Jules had big doe eyes that kicked him in the gut every time she looked his way. "Hey, don't you do the employee vetting on all the hires here?"

Declan worked for McKay-Taggart, a security services firm that provided everything from investigative pros to bodyguards to background checks. Top and MT were tied together since they were both owned by Taggarts. Chef Sean Taggart had left MT to start his restaurant empire and Ian Taggart had funded him with MT money. Big Tag, as they called him, came in several times a week, and the dude could eat.

But Javier kind of thought the tiny brunette ate more. He watched as she said something to Jules that made her smile. She had a bunch of daily menus held to her chest, her good hand covering her prosthetic. She did that a lot. She hid that hand or tried to cover it with something. She tried not to use it and it made her life hard.

Didn't he know a thing or two about stubborn vets?

"Yeah, I ran some of the applications," Declan replied. His eyes were narrowed, but he took a long drink of the beer in front of him. "You think I missed something?"

Javier should have known that was where he would go. "Dude, you've got to stop being pessimistic. You always go to the worst place."

Declan shrugged. "If you always go to the worst place, you got nowhere else to go but up. I don't get optimists, man. It's like setting yourself up to fall. If you always think everything is shit and it's all going to hell, then you can be pleasantly surprised when it works out for the best."

Linc nodded. "Yeah, that seems like a good life philosophy."

Javier shook his head. "No, it's a terrible one. What happened to the two of you?"

"Lots of stuff," Linc replied. "I got shot to shit in Iraq and Dec here keeps getting the worst headaches, and he has some weird dreams, I think."

Dec shot Linc the finger. "I don't need you to play doctor. I need you to pour me another beer."

Javier could have told him the beer wasn't going to help with a headache, but Declan didn't look like a man ready to take advice. "And I was only asking because I'm curious about the new girl."

Linc glanced toward the dining room. "The one with the crazy eyes?"

Sometimes he was certain Linc sampled the product too much. Other times he was aware that the big guy was a massive puppy who'd been kicked one too many times. He could still love a good pet from time to time, but he was capable of biting the hand that fed him. Linc had a metal plate in his head that made him near impossible to deal with at airports, and a load of shitty memories that made him go a little crazy from time to time.

"No, buddy. I was talking about Jules." Jules, with the sad eyes and that crazy waterfall of red hair he thought about getting caught in. Like she was some gorgeous mermaid and her hair caught men and brought them in for the kill.

It might be a good way to go.

Declan turned, setting down the beer he'd been nursing. He'd come in the last few nights to hang out and start to get what he called a "feel" for the place. Javier wasn't sure Top had a "feel," but apparently it was important since they were hosting an up-and-coming country-western singer soon and Declan and the bodyguards were providing security. Javier kind of thought Dec had taken lead on the job for the free food and beer. "You interested in Jules?"

If by interested Dec meant couldn't get her out of his head, Javier was interested.

But he wasn't about to say anything so…touchy, feely. He wasn't one of those guys. Nope. The kind who talked about their feelings and had feelings. Did he have feelings? He wasn't sure. Oh, he was good with anger and irritation. Lately, he wasn't so good with happiness or joy.

"I'm curious about her. She doesn't talk a lot to the guys. I managed to find out that she was in the Navy. Eric served with her ex-husband and that's how she got the job, but other than telling me how to cook, she's pretty closed down." Except sometimes she would laugh and her whole face would brighten. "She shows up in my life a lot lately. I wonder about her."

"She shows up in your life?" Dec asked, suddenly getting serious. "You think she's stalking you for some reason? Damn, man. I told you that dick of yours was going to get you in trouble. I didn't actually run her application, but I'll pull it and go back through her history. Do you think you had one of your encounters with her and she's pissed?"

Sometimes it sucked to be surrounded by worst-case scenario guys. He held up his hands. "No. Absolutely not. She's not stalking me. She moved in to the apartment across the hall. Eric asked if I knew of a place and it opened up. She certainly didn't come looking for me. And she rehabs at the same center I take Rafael to. I've seen her talking to him but when I ask what they were talking about he tells me to mind my own business."

"You think she's moving in on your brother?" Linc asked.

He hadn't even considered that. He didn't like the thought. Not at all. Still, she hadn't seemed flirty with Rafe. "First of all, she gave me the name of the rehab center. It wasn't like she followed us there. And I don't think she's moving in on Rafe. No woman with half a brain would touch my toxic as shit brother right now. No. She was being kind to him. Not that he deserves it. I'm curious about her. She seems to know her way around a kitchen far better than any newbie hostess I've met."

"That's because she's Annaliese O'Neil's daughter," Linc said.

Dec frowned his way. "How the fuck did you know that? I was told to keep that quiet."

Linc shrugged, one shoulder moving negligently. "I like her show. She's got a soothing voice and she has some very good tips when it comes to cocktails. Also, there's a picture of her daughter in her biography. It's Jules. If Jules knows something about cooking, it's because she was raised by her mom."

"You read some decorator's bio?" Dec shook his head like he

was trying to get the image out.

"I can read," Linc shot back. "Mostly comic books and gaming magazines, but you know what—I'm single and I don't want to live in squalor. Her notes on feng shui really improved my sleep patterns."

Well, he was not going to judge a book by its outwardly masculine cover anymore. He needed to spend more time with Linc. Dude was a trip. "So she's like an heiress or something? What's she doing in my rathole building?"

"I don't know what happened," Dec admitted. "But I know she needed this job. She seems like a nice lady. She's not your usual."

Javier turned and Jules was frowning down at the brunette. It was obvious that conversation had gone wrong. He didn't like the way Jules had paled. He slipped off his barstool, and tipped his glass her way. Maybe she would come over and have a drink with them. "Yeah, I know. I don't think I have a usual anymore."

Nope. Jules merely nodded his way and went back to the kitchen.

Dec's brows rose. "That's not what I heard. I heard you went on quite a tear."

He felt himself flush. "I was stupid. You know how some guys get bad news and go on a bender? Yeah, I sometimes do that with sex."

"Because of all the shit with Rafe?" Linc asked.

Javier couldn't look him in the eye. He stared at his beer. "Yeah. About a month ago I decided to try, really try to settle down with a woman. Thought I found a good one. The night I was going to ask her to be my sub, Rafe showed up. She bailed as fast as she could. So instead of a pretty sub to take care of me, I get to take care of my brother, who hates everything and everyone. For a couple of weeks there I would put his ass to bed and call some women I knew. It wasn't like they were looking for relationships, if you know what I mean. I'm sleeping on a pullout bed in the living room. It was all about sex."

It was all about forgetting his shitastic existence for a few hours.

"Hey, no one is blaming you, man," Dec replied. "I talked to Rafe for about two minutes before I realized I would rather punch him than listen to him. He's pretty rough right now. Do you want me to look into those friends of his?"

"I would like to bar them from the apartment building, but then Rafe manages to get his ass out on the street, and that goes poorly, too." He wasn't sure what to do. One minute Rafe was apologizing and promising to be better. The next he was trying to punch a guy at the grocery store who he said was giving him the eye or something.

"Let me check 'em out," Dec encouraged. "I got nothing better to do with my time."

"Sure. That would be great. I'm just grateful that Rafe changed his mind about the surgery. He's having a procedure in the morning that should help manage his pain. He's having trouble with the prosthetics. This is supposed to make it easier for him to walk in them. I'm not sure if that's a good thing or not. He'll be able to get his own booze or whatever."

"I thought he said he wouldn't do it." Linc nodded as the brunette walked by. The one with the slightly crazy eyes. "Good evening, ma'am."

She waved and that was when he realized she wasn't looking at Linc. It was Dec who had her attention. She stared at him for a moment before hurrying out the door.

Top was closed for the night.

"Jules talked him into it." He put his beer down, ready to put some tables together for supper. "I'm brother free for a few days and I have her to thank for it."

And for his recent celibacy. He'd caught her watching as one of his fuck buddies said good-bye one morning. He hadn't liked her seeing that part of him.

It was weird and he wasn't sure what to do about it.

"You going to grab the grub? I'm starving." Linc pulled his apron off.

Dec slid off his barstool. "I could totally eat."

Yeah he was here for "work." Javier started for the kitchen, but the other chefs were already bringing out the food while Ally and Tiff set the table.

Since he didn't have a houseguest, shouldn't he think about having someone over? Indulge in his drug of choice? He could have sex in his own bed for once.

He pushed through the doors and caught sight of her. Jules was talking to Grace Taggart, her hair pulled back. She smiled at something Grace said.

Or maybe he could try something different for a change. Maybe he could try something new.

God knew he could use it.

Chapter Two

Jules frowned down at the paper. Her handwriting sucked, and it looked even worse next to her grandmother's super-neat script. Of course, her grandma had use of her dominant hand and Jules was trying to make do with her right hand.

Making do. Wasn't that exactly what she was trying to do?

That's what her mom would call the cookbook. *Making Do – How to Cook with One Hand Tied Behind Your Back*—or left somewhere in Iraq.

It was just an experiment. She'd found a box filled with her grandma's recipes in the stuff Kevin had sent her from their old place in South Carolina. The recipes were the everyday food a housewife would cook. It was far too plebeian for her mother's show. Many of the ingredients were canned or staples of a cupboard. Easy to put together.

Maybe easy to cook with one hand.

She'd been making a few notes on Slow Cooker Stuffed Bell Peppers.

The key was trying to figure out how to use a knife with a hand she still felt clumsy with.

Thunder shook her little space.

Damn, something was going on outside. She glanced out the window and rain was coming down in sheets.

It would be a long night. She didn't like storms. Storms made her remember.

Her cell phone trilled and she saw the number flash. Ah, the cavalry. She had to smile as she ran her finger across the screen. "Hello, Doc. How are you?"

Kai Ferguson's voice came over the line, smooth and peaceful. "Well, I was calling to ask you the very same question."

It was good to have someone give a shit about her. "It's just a storm. I'll be good."

"Jules, you don't have to be strong. You nearly died in a storm. You lost your hand and it hasn't been very long since that night. It's all right to be afraid," he said. "Kori was wondering if you might want to come over for dinner and a movie."

Kori Ferguson was as kick ass as her husband. Though Jules hadn't been in town long, she'd been more than happy to find a place where she didn't feel like a freak. That was one of the best things about Top. Chef chose to hire as many veterans as he could, and he didn't care how many limbs they came with. Or rather, he really did because he immediately offered his employees Kai's services. But she was an adult and it was time to stop flinching when the thunder rolled in. "I can't tell you how much I appreciate it, Kai, but I need to do this."

"All right, then. Did you think about what we talked about on Thursday? I ask because there's a play party coming up at a place I trust. If you would like to go I would send you with an instructional Dom to test the waters and see if it's something you're interested in."

Ah, the BDSM question. It was one of the perks of being a Top employee, though the trainee program was shut down for a few months. They'd reached capacity, but there would always be people moving in and out. She'd indicated she was interested and Kai took that seriously.

Was she interested? Kind of, but she wasn't even sure if she would be a top or a bottom. Still, what the hell else was she doing with her life? "Would he know about me? You know, about my arm?"

There was a slight pause that let her know Kai was dealing with her carefully. "Yes, if you like I would make sure he knew. Though you should understand I would never choose someone who would reject you. This is a training relationship."

She winced. He was right. This Dom wouldn't be looking to date her. It wasn't a sexual thing. It was a very polite agreement to show her around and talk to her about what she saw and felt. "Forget I said anything. Seriously, Kai, I wasn't thinking. Anyone you would recommend is great. I would like very much to go."

"Excellent. I'll send you all the information tomorrow. And again, if you find it's hard to get through tonight, call us. We're watching some sort of horror film about sharks. You would be saving me."

"I'll remember that. Thanks, Kai." She hung up with him.

The lightning flashed and thunder shook the building. She took a deep breath. A long and lonely night. It would be all right. She would find a movie to watch and get cozy on the couch. Maybe a romance.

The night before she'd sat next to Javier at family dinner. He'd been polite, talking to her about how well the sauce had gone and asking questions about her background.

He'd been attentive, his focus on her. He'd made sure she had everything she needed and then he'd walked her back to their apartment building just two blocks away.

It had been a long time since she'd had a man pay that much attention to her. Not since she and Kevin had started dating. It had been nice at first, and then when she'd realized how invested she was getting in a single conversation with the man, a little unnerving.

She'd found herself giggling and flirting and she'd had to shut that shit down.

She wasn't sure what Javier was doing by spending so much time with her, but she needed time to think about it.

Another blast of lightning and then thunder that shook the world around her. Well, she would have time tonight since there was zero chance she was sleeping through this. She would be up all night long.

She reached for her pencil. With her left hand.

God, when would she stop doing that? It had been eighteen months and she still reached out like her hand was there, like she could pick up the pencil and easily write down her ideas on tweaking the spices the way she used to with her mom's recipes. When would it become natural to remember that her left hand was gone? To not feel it?

When she dreamed at night she could cook. She was the chef, her knife moving with consummate ease, chopping with perfect precision.

And then she woke up and could barely open a can of coffee without making a mess.

She needed a distraction. Hopefully there was a movie on TV.

The lights went out, everything going quiet and still.

Shit.

She waited for a moment. Come on. Turn back on.

Nothing.

She'd paid her bill. It couldn't be that. Jules got up and went to the window. Yep. Everything was dark up and down the block. They'd blown a transformer somewhere.

All alone with the storm. Maybe she should call Kai. And ask him to get out in the middle of this? That seemed pretty selfish, especially since she knew exactly how poorly traveling through storms could go.

A hard flash of white light made her jump back.

Nope. She wasn't going there. She was going to stay in the here and now, and that meant finding a flashlight and trying to get some candles lit. Someone was out there working on getting the power back on, and then she would ride out the storm watching rom coms and falling asleep on the couch. It was going to be okay. Deep breath. It was going to be okay.

A few moments later she'd found her one flashlight and had a nice set of candles out, and she was faced with the problem of lighting the suckers. Oh, she had a big box of matches, but she'd never struck a match without her left hand.

A lighter would be easier. She could figure out a lighter maybe. Jules tried holding the box against the table with her stump while she struck the match with her right hand. She fumbled, the action so unnatural it made her slip up and break the match.

And the second one.

And the third one.

Tears pierced her eyes, but she wasn't going to shed them. She was going to figure this out or she would make do with the flashlight. It was all about adapting. That was what she had to do. Adapt.

She wasn't going to let this beat her. Normally she was tough. The accident had happened and she dealt with it. She didn't feel the need to sit down and cry when she had trouble opening a can or working her phone. But between the storm and the conversation with Suzanne the day before about her mother and the sweetness of flirting with a handsome man she couldn't have, she was feeling particularly vulnerable.

Jules took a deep breath. She wasn't going to sit here in the dark and cry.

A knock on the door made her gasp and jump.

Fuck. She wasn't like this. She hated this…this anxiety she got when it rained. It was weakness and she couldn't abide it.

If you walk away from this you'll ruin your life, Juliana. Don't think I'll watch you do it. You go through with this and you do it on your own. Am I understood?

Sometimes she felt like she was still seven years old, and if she could just get her mom's attention everything would be okay.

Jules gripped the flashlight and walked across her apartment to the door. It was likely one of the neighbors coming to check on her. Actually, that was an excellent idea. She could go down and see if Mrs. Gleeson needed some company. There were some elderly residents she could check on and a single mom she'd met at the end of the hall. She could see if she could be of any assistance and that would get her through the night.

She opened the door expecting to see anyone but the man she saw standing there.

Javier Leones. He had a flashlight in one hand and a bottle of wine in the other. He was wearing jeans and a button down that he'd left undone enough she could see a nice swath of golden brown skin. His hair was deliciously mussed, as though he'd taken a shower and simply rubbed a towel over it to get it dry.

He was big and male and so sexy it hurt to look at him, and Jules realized she could do something else to take her mind off things.

Those plump, sensual lips of his broke into a bright smile. "I thought you might like some company. I know I would. I actually don't have any candles. I was sitting in my living room with this one sad flashlight. You look like a woman who has some candles."

But she couldn't light them. She hadn't figured that part out.

His face fell and he walked into her place, closing and locking the door behind him. "Hey, what's wrong? It's okay if you don't have any candles. It's cool. Two flashlights are better than one."

He set the flashlight and wine bottle down and moved into her space, his hands coming up to cup her shoulders. "Jules, what's wrong?"

She had to be stronger than this. She shook her head. "Nothing. I'm fine."

His jaw tightened. "Don't. Please don't. I live with a stubborn asshole who won't let me help him in any way. I get that we've only known each other for a few weeks, but I thought we were friends. You help me out all the time. You're kind to me. Fucking let me be kind to you. Please let me feel like I'm worth something."

If he'd said anything else, joked about the weather or told her to suck it up, she could have, but he'd opened a door. He'd been vulnerable and honest, and she found she couldn't pay that back with stubbornness.

"I have plenty of candles and I can't figure out how to light them." Tears rolled down her face. She *was* vulnerable. All the time. Even when she pretended like she wasn't.

"You can't..." he began and then he looked down. Instead of stepping back and giving her space, he drew his hand down her arm, warming her skin where he touched her. It was dark but the moon was full and gave enough light to see the outline of his face. There was no look of horror there. He caressed her arm until he got to the place where she'd been split apart and sewn back together unwhole. He brought it up and wrapped it against his palm, his fingers closing around it until the whole thing was surrounded with his warmth. "You haven't figured out how to do it yet. Probably hasn't come up or you would know what to do. How long since you lost your hand?"

"A year and a half," she said. He was touching her there. No one had touched her there except her doctors and therapists.

Come to think of it, no one had touched her at all since before the accident. Had it really been so long since she'd felt warm flesh against her own? He was close, close enough that all she would have to do was go up on her toes to brush her lips against his.

Would that be wrong? As long as she remembered who she was dealing with, why couldn't she take a few moments of respite for herself? If he wanted her.

He stepped back, letting go of her arm and leaving her colder than she'd been before. "I have no doubt that you can figure out how to make it work, but let me help out tonight. Like I said, I spend all my time with a cranky vet."

He had the flashlight back in his hand and he quickly found the candles and matches.

"How is Rafe doing?" She needed to slow down because she wasn't even sure she was his type. Though his type seemed to be female and willing.

Was she really going to suggest that they go at it?

He lit the first match, touching it to one of the candles and then another. "His surgery went well. They're keeping him until Wednesday. I'm hoping that he won't be in as much pain after the procedure and that will spur him to actually try in his rehab sessions."

"I know it sucks at first, but it's one of those things that gets easier the more you do it," she said, watching him move the candles around until they lit the whole room. Yeah, the light did not take anything away from how lovely he was. "Using the prosthetics, though obviously it's a long process. I'm not entirely comfortable with mine. It hurts sometimes. I'm clumsy with it so I try to do a lot without it."

"Yours is body powered?" Javier asked, setting the last of the candles down.

He knew a lot, but then he had a brother who'd been through it all. "Yes, I chose the body powered over electric."

"Why? The electric would be more functional."

"It's also way more expensive," she replied.

He seemed about to say something, but then let it go. "How'd you lose it? If you don't mind my asking."

Somehow she didn't with him. He was part of the "family," so to speak. "I jumped in the water to save this family that had been fleeing… I don't even know if they were fleeing us or the bad guys. You know it's all relative in the middle of battle when you're a civilian. They were on this raft thing and it was coming apart. I went out with a team to save them. It was storming and dark. We could barely see them. You don't want to be out on the water in a storm in that gulf, let me tell you. We were supposed to stay in the boat; try to save them, but stay in the boat. I couldn't. I jumped in and managed to save the six-year-old, but when I was trying to climb back in the boat we got hit by a wave and I was tossed off. I was in all the right gear and everyone did the right things, but at some point, that raft came undone and I got smacked with it. Nearly drowned and ended up cutting the hell out of my hand on one of the nails they used. Went to the infirmary after a hard-core dressing down and that was where I picked up the staph infection. I left a good portion of my arm behind, got a discharge, and the rest is history."

"That's rough. Can I stay for a while? I did bring wine. I hope you like Pinot," he said, holding up the bottle.

"There's a corkscrew in the drawer next to the dishwasher. I can open a bottle of wine with one hand," she admitted. "I taught myself how to do that really fast."

"I like a woman who has her priorities straight." He quickly found the corkscrew. "Hopefully this doesn't go on for long, but the last time we lost power it was four or five hours. Do you mind if I hang out here? I'm not much of a loner."

"I don't like storms so I don't mind the company at all." She opened the cabinet and found a couple of wine glasses.

He poured like a man who had taken many a shift at the bar. "I can imagine it reminds you. Let's talk about something else. How did you get into the business?"

Wow, something she wanted to talk about even less than how she lost her hand. "I got the job at Top because I knew Eric. He was actually closer to my ex-husband, but we were all friendly. When I got out, Kevin called him and asked about a job."

He handed her the glass. "You're friendly with your ex?"

So many subjects she didn't like to talk about. What did that say about her? She was getting closed off to the world and people around her—what would be left? "I guess we went into the marriage more as friends than anything else. We were both in the Navy. It seemed like the right thing to do at the time. When I left the Navy, suddenly the marriage wasn't right for him anymore. I don't blame him. It wasn't a super passionate thing."

And she'd liked it that way. It had been comfortable. She hadn't been devastated when he'd left, hadn't sat and cried for days like her mother had. Like she had when her father left. The divorce with Kevin had gone as smoothly as their marriage had most of the time. It had proven to her that she was right. People came together when it worked for them and broke apart the minute it didn't. Being practical was important.

Javier leaned against the bar. "Really? Not a true love kind of girl, huh?"

"If there is such a thing, I haven't found it," she admitted.

"Why do you think people get married then? Why do some of them stay together for life? My parents did. My mama still mourns my papa." He was staring at her, obviously waiting to see what she would say.

She wasn't going to get into an argument with him. If his parents had managed to stick it out for life then good for them. "Funny, I wouldn't think you would be the one to argue for true love."

He winced. "I'm not as bad as my reputation might seem. I will admit I've done my fair share of partying, but I've had some relationships. I'm not against having another one if the right person came along."

This felt much better than talking about her. "Did blondie come back?"

He sighed and took a drink. "Yeah, you were right on point about her. She ran as fast as she could the minute I had more responsibility than driving her home from a night of fun. I'm pretty sure she was only interested in me for connections to Sanctum."

"I thought Sanctum membership was closed." That was what she'd been told.

"Not exactly. They're not running training classes right now. Big Tag doesn't want the club to get too full. There are a lot of very powerful people who play at Sanctum and they get nervous when there are too many people around."

"He sounds a little like a mobster." She'd seen the man but hadn't actually talked to him. Big Tag didn't wait to be seated. There was a table that was always held open for him and he knew the way.

"I think Big Tag would say he knows the power of influence. He wouldn't ever use a person's sexual proclivities against them, but it does give him the chance to sit at the bar with some people who can do his business an enormous amount of good," Javier explained.

Rather like her mother. Her mother could work a relationship like no one she'd ever seen. Right up to the point that relationship became inconvenient.

A clap of thunder shook the house and she jumped.

Javier put down the glass and moved to her again, his hands on her arms. "Hey, it's okay. You really don't like storms."

She hated being weak. "I'm good."

"Sweetheart, you're shaking." He took the glass out of her hand and drew her in, wrapping his arms around her. "It's okay. Let me take care of you. You helped me out that night, and don't think I don't see you trying to help my brother. I'll stay with you. You don't have to worry."

Those big arms came around her and she was completely enveloped in his warmth. She knew she should step back. She had to work with this man, but she couldn't. He felt way too good. She liked him. He was a nice guy, and according to rumors he'd slept with coworkers before and hadn't had a problem with them afterward. A couple of waitresses, one of the hostesses who'd moved on.

He'd come looking for her. He'd come with wine and now he was giving her physical attention. Surely that meant he'd come over looking for some attention himself.

It wasn't wrong to tilt her head up, to look up at that gorgeous face of his. Somehow in the candlelight it felt right to hold on to him.

He looked down at her and she caught the moment he went from "guy giving girl comfort" to "guy who might get some comfort of his own." His eyes seemed to darken, the arms around her tightening slightly like he didn't want to let her get away. "Juliana, you shouldn't look at me like that, sweetheart."

"Why shouldn't I?" She couldn't stop staring at his lips. It had been too damn long since a man had kissed her.

"Because it could get you in trouble. It could make me think things I shouldn't."

Yes, this was what she needed. There was zero question he was rejecting her. He'd come here for this, for her. It didn't mean more than they both needed someone tonight and that was okay. "What would you think? What would you think if I went on my toes and did this?"

She pressed up and brushed her lips over his, an easy affection. It was over almost before it began, but she felt a shudder go through his big body.

"Yeah, that might make me think about doing this," he whispered before his arms moved, hands coming up to cup the sides of her face. His fingertips brushed over her skin before he tightened his hold and dipped his head down. His mouth covered hers, lips aligning with perfection.

He moved his mouth on hers, easing into the kiss. He took his time, gentle at first, and then she felt the warmth of his tongue requesting entry. There was no way she would keep him out. Somewhere in the background she could hear the rain pounding against the roof, but it wasn't a thing to be afraid of now. Now it made the world seem cozy and safe. She wasn't alone for the night. She didn't even have to contemplate it. No worries, just this.

His tongue slid, dancing with hers. She let him lead, giving over completely because it felt good to not be in charge. He showed her how to move, gently nudging her this way or that.

When he moved away, she was breathless.

He stared down at her as though memorizing her face. The man knew how to make a woman feel like she was the center of the world. She could see why women fell in line to wait for a chance to spend the night with him.

"I didn't intend to do this tonight," he said, one side of his mouth curling up in the sexiest grin she'd ever seen.

"But you intended to do it?" She hadn't missed his wording.

He smoothed her hair down before running his hands along her back and bringing their bodies together.

Damn but that felt good. Her skin was heating up, nipples starting to peak. Her brain was going a little fuzzy and it had nothing at all to do with the wine.

"Yes, I did," he admitted, his voice low and deep. He leaned over and kissed her on the forehead, moving down toward her nose. Each caress was soft and sweet. "I knew I was going to try to seduce you fairly early on. I have to admit I've been a little obsessed with you these last few weeks. You're very different from other women I've known."

He brushed his mouth over hers and then kissed along her jaw.

She could barely get the question out. "How am I different? Not as blonde as your usual?"

"I don't have a type like that, sweetheart." His lips trailed to her ear, licking over the shell and making her shiver. "I tend to like my women fun and easy, and I think you're more interesting than that. I think you're complex. I think you could be very satisfying."

She *knew* he would be satisfying. "Why don't you kiss me again and we'll find out?"

"Oh, I knew you would be a righteous brat." He said the words, but there was a deep amusement to his voice that made her think he was okay with that.

Brat. She kind of liked the word. She'd been damn near perfect as a child. It had only been coming out of high school that she'd felt a real need to break away. To leave all of it behind and do something she'd never done before.

It was time to break away again, time to find a new her, and this felt like a damn fine place to start.

He lowered his head down and kissed her again. This time his intention was plain. He surged into her mouth, his tongue rubbing against hers. Long and slow and infinitely carnal. His hands moved over her body and before she really knew what was happening, she found herself lifting her arms and letting him draw the tank top over her head, exposing her breasts. He turned her, bringing her back up against his front. Those big hands ran up her body and cupped her breasts.

"I knew they would be beautiful. Look at how perfect they are in my hands. Do you see how we fit together?" His mouth was against her ear, the words hot and sweet. "I took one look at you and knew we would fit together just like this."

Oh, he was good. Brilliant. This was what it meant to have her body played by a master. No one had ever kissed her the way Javier did—like she was the sweetest fruit and he couldn't get enough of her. She let her head fall back against his chest. "I know this feels good."

"It feels right." He seemed content for a moment to touch her breasts, learning their shape and firmness. He kissed the shell of her ear, licked along it until he got to the lobe, where he gave her a playful nip.

She gasped and shuddered in his arms because that little nip of pain had gone straight through her body to her pussy. She was wet and warm down there. What normally took forever with her ex, Javier managed to do with a couple of kisses and some hot words. "I think we should take this to my bedroom."

One hand came up, shifting her hair to the side. "You move fast, sweetheart. I like to take my time. I think I probably have more experience than you, so maybe I should take the lead here. You see, I think you're greedy, baby. I think you want me to hop on top of you and get you off as fast as I can."

"Not sure what's wrong with that."

"What's wrong with that is everything. I told you I had plans for you and I'm not going to change them because the timetable moved up."

"Plans?"

"Plans to take all night. Plans to go slow and make this last. Plans to show you how good this can be." He kissed her shoulder, his free hand starting to inch down her body toward the waistband of her pajama bottoms. "I can't do that with a quickie. Tell me how long it's been."

There was a decadent bite of command in his voice that really did something for her. Still, she found herself fighting him a little. "What makes you think it's been a while?"

His fingers dipped inside her pajama bottoms, inching ever closer to the place that seemed to have become the center of her world. "Let's see. I know I'm a pretty boy, but I have a brain, too. Don't underestimate me. I've been around the McKay-Taggart boys long enough to know how to deduce a few things about the people near me. One—you recently divorced. Couples who have excellent sex on a regular basis don't tend to divorce. Two—your husband was also military and you were both deployed. Even if you were having good sex, distance would be a problem, and I don't think you're the kind to play around while you're married."

"No playing around." Was that her voice? It was breathy and sexy. She couldn't quite catch a deep breath because those fingers of his were playing at the edges of her pussy, coming close to her clitoris. Poor, lonely clitoris.

Yeah, masturbation hadn't been the same since she lost her

dominant hand.

"Then there's the third part." He whispered the words against her ear, quiet and low, like they were only ever meant to be heard by her. "You went through something traumatic. You probably haven't felt sexy in a long time."

"Not in forever, Javier." She was vulnerable, wanted to believe this was something real, but it wasn't. He was a good-time guy who knew how to work a woman. She had to remember that at all times and take the good he had to give her.

He wasn't trying to hurt her. This was simply what he did, and when she looked at it in a positive fashion, it was all right. He hadn't promised her a thing. He was bringing her pleasure and making her feel like a woman again. In the morning she would thank him and never give him a moment's worth of awkwardness.

He was exactly what she needed.

"You are the single, sexiest thing I've seen in forever," he said as his finger made that first light pass over her clit.

Her vision went soft. Yeah, the storm couldn't touch her here. "I don't know, Javi. I've seen some of your conquests and you like them beautiful."

"It's not the same." The hand on her breast began to move, lightly pinching her nipple between his thumb and forefinger. "You're different. You're gorgeous, but there's something more about you. Not a single one of those women I've spent time with lately would have been kind to my brother."

"Then you choose crappy women."

"I didn't choose them for their personalities. I chose them because they didn't want anything out of me. Not anything other than sex. Do you understand, Juliana?"

He was offering her sex and nothing more. She could handle that even though her heart was already softening toward him. He was being honest and that was all she could ask of him. But she was a big girl and she wasn't looking for another relationship. She wasn't good at them. This, though, this she could handle. This she could crave.

"I understand." She could barely hear the words over the pulse pounding through her.

A single finger ran over her clit, pressing with just enough force to make her gasp and try to squirm.

He held her tight. "Good. I want to make things clear between us. You're different. You should know that. And I know you're eager. I know you want this and you want it now. I do, too, but I know how good it can be when we take our time. But, sweetheart, that doesn't mean I can't give you a little taste. Do you want that?"

She nodded. "Yes. I want that. I want you, Javier."

Even if he would break her heart at the end. Feeling like this—even briefly—was worth it. Her life had been bleak since that night, colorless and bland. Now she felt vibrant, spicy, and a little on the wild side. She was old enough to know feeling like this had a price and that price was heartache, but she would manage it. Anything was better than how dull she felt every day of her life.

"I want you, too." That finger of his picked up the pace and she couldn't help but rub herself against him like a damn cat in heat. It didn't matter because she could feel his cock hard against her ass. He wanted her. He wasn't scared off by her missing limb or how she could put her nose in where it didn't belong. He wanted her.

She relaxed for the first time in forever and gave over to him. He was the one with the experience and she let him have his way.

The orgasm broke over her, a wave she didn't want to cage. Jules didn't hold back, moaning over the steady sound of rain.

When the thunder rattled the apartment this time, she barely noticed.

* * * *

Javier felt the orgasm go through her and a real thrill of pleasure spilled across him. He'd watched her carefully over the weeks she'd been at Top and he would bet a lot that Juliana O'Neil wasn't a woman who gave over easily. It would be hard for her to let go and forget about her problems, but she'd given in to him without a whisper of trouble.

Because she felt what he did. She had to feel that this was right. For the first freaking time in his life, he was with the right woman.

One good thing. That was all he needed. The last several weeks of his life had been past difficult, but if he came out of it with Jules by his side and in his bed, it would all be worth it. He could handle Rafael's damage as long as he had Jules.

"Take these off for me." There was no reason for her to keep those pajama bottoms and undies on. He pushed them off her hips and she managed to kick them away.

He leaned over and picked her up, carrying her to the couch.

Her eyes were soft and a bit hazy when she looked up at him. "Shouldn't we go to the bedroom?"

He loved how husky her voice had gone. That whiskey rough voice went straight to his dick. Not that he needed more encouragement. He was hard as hell as it was. "No light in there and I want to see you. I want to see every inch of that gorgeous body."

She flushed slightly and shifted her damaged arm. She talked a good game, but it was obvious it bothered her.

"Don't." He gently gripped her arm and brought it up to his lips. There was nothing wrong with her. Even her scars were beautiful. He kissed the place where they'd taken a piece of her. "This is beautiful, too, sweetheart. This is sacrifice and love. Don't ever try to hide it."

"You're killing me, Javier," she said. "You know exactly what to say."

He often didn't. He often fumbled, but it seemed to come easy with her. Most of the women he'd been with, there hadn't been a ton of talking. He knew what his reputation was. Hell, he'd nurtured it for years. If a lady wanted a good time, he was her guy. No strings. No promises. Most of the time no repeats, though he'd broken that rule on occasion. He moved fast and always left his lovers satisfied. He was Hurricane Javier. He got in, got the job done, and walked away before it got too heavy. Sometimes that meant walking away before names were exchanged.

Something had changed over the last few months. Maybe it had been watching his friends settle down, but damn it, he wanted more and he wanted it with this woman.

He wanted what Macon had with Ally. What Eric and Deena had found. What Sebastian and Tiffany had.

Her couch was big and comfy. He could do what he needed to do. He kissed her once more and then dragged his shirt over his head. Skin to skin. He wanted to feel her warmth around him.

He was always open and honest with women. He told them what he was willing to give. Telling Jules she was different from other women felt right.

Everything felt right with her.

For the first time in his life he was in deep with a woman.

Her skin was warm, practically glowing in the candlelight. She was a sexy goddess lying there waiting for him, her nipples tight and skin flushed. He could see how her pussy glistened from the orgasm he'd given her. It made his cock tighten even further until he was almost certain the damn thing was going to break out and try to get inside her on its own.

"Take them off, Javier," she demanded. "I want to see you. I've thought long and hard about what you would look like without all those clothes."

She'd thought about him, had she? He couldn't help the fact that her words made him feel about ten feet tall. It made all the time he spent in the gym worth it. He unbuckled his belt and shoved his jeans down, toeing out of his sneakers. He tossed them to the side but not before fishing out the condom he kept in his wallet. Just in case.

"You're a Boy Scout," she said, looking him over. "A big, gorgeous, always prepared Boy Scout."

"I'm an optimist." He laid the condom on the coffee table and dropped to his knees. "But you can change your mind at any time. I'm willing to take this slow if you want to. I can be patient when it comes to you."

She reached for him. "I don't need patience. I need more."

Oh, he could give her so much more. He needed more, too. He dipped his head down and took one of those tight nipples into his mouth, sucking her hard. He felt a shiver go through her and her hand found his hair, sinking in and holding him there.

"It's been so fucking long," she whispered. "Please don't stop. It feels good."

When they'd settled into whatever this was going to become, he would slowly introduce her to D/s. She would never want a full-time submissive role, but she would enjoy it in the bedroom. She'd given over perfectly to him the minute he'd taken control. She was reacting to him beautifully, her needs seeming to dovetail with his own.

He could have plenty of vanilla sex, but any relationship would have a touch of kink. He needed it. It was time to leave the party boy behind and get serious about life. It was odd to think he'd been hesitantly ready to test the waters with Kristy a few weeks back. That had been a mistake he'd been saved from. He'd been cautious with her, wanting the relationship more than the woman herself. He couldn't say that about Jules. There was no caution with her. He was jumping right in the deep end with this woman.

He moved to the other breast, laving it with affection. When he was ready, he started moving down her body, kissing and licking as he began to make his way to his final destination. "I'm glad to hear you think about me because I haven't been able to get my mind off you since that night you came and saved me with Rafe. Did I thank you for that?"

"I consider this a proper thank you," she replied. "I'm surprised you had time to think about me with all those women coming in and out of your place."

He winced, kissing her belly button and letting his tongue play there. "That was me sliding back into bad behavior."

She shook her head. "No apologies. I don't hold that against you, Javi."

They hadn't been together then. Now they were. "You truly are perfect. Do you know what I thought about most? I thought about how you would taste. I thought about getting my mouth right here."

He covered her pussy with his mouth and had to hold her down when she nearly came off the couch.

This was what he'd wanted to do, hold her down and make a

meal out of her. He moved between her legs, making a place for himself. He settled in and spread her labia gently, not wanting to miss an inch of her flesh. He glanced up her body, loving how her head was thrown back in pure ecstasy.

He eased a finger inside her while his tongue worked her clit. Tight. She was going to grip his dick like a vise. He wouldn't last long once he was in there, but he could make sure she was primed and ready to go over the edge with him.

He curled a finger inside her, every ounce of his focus on her response. He wanted to learn exactly how to touch her, how she liked to be licked, where she needed him to suck her softly or pull her flesh into his mouth with purpose.

They would have plenty of time. After Rafe came home, he would be able to settle his brother in for the night and then sneak over here to be with her. Having her close would be a godsend.

This was how he planned to spend his nights. Right here between her legs. He sucked on her clit and he was glad the storm was loud because there would have been no way their neighbors didn't hear her screaming out his name.

He came up on his knees and stroked himself, rolling the condom on. There was no reason to wait. He could take her and start this out right.

"You're gorgeous everywhere, aren't you, Leones?" Jules wrapped her legs around his waist. "And you're every bit what was advertised."

A little alarm rang through his system, but she pressed her pelvis up, sliding her pussy along his cock, and he let the thought float away. All that mattered was getting inside her. This was what everyone had talked about. When it was right, it was easy to sink in and give over.

He pressed inside. She was tight, but so wet he needed little force. Still, she held on to him and he eased his way, thrusting in and pulling out in short bursts. He took her inch by inch until she had all of him. Her nails dug into his back, the pain lighting him up as he thrust with purpose. He let himself go because he could feel she was close again. He pressed his body into her, rotating and hitting her clit with every powerful thrust.

Her eyes went wide as she came again and Javier fucked her hard. Every bit of his focus was on one thing, bringing her as much pleasure as he could before the inevitable happened. Her head fell back and she moaned again.

He couldn't hold out any longer. It was too good. He felt the tingle at the base of his spine and then he was the one who was shouting over the storm. Pleasure coursed through his body and when he was done, he fell against her, completely weak.

Her hand stroked down his back as he came down from the high.

"That was exactly what I needed," she said with a husky chuckle.

It was what he needed, too. He cuddled close and realized how long he'd waited for this woman. He'd thought it would be hard to deal with, but Eric had been one hundred percent correct. When the woman was right, giving in was easy.

Javier laid his head on her breast. Pretty breast. "When I've got some strength again, I'll move us to the bed and prove that you haven't had everything you need yet."

"I'll hold you to that," she replied.

That was exactly what he was counting on.

Chapter Three

Javier woke up to the warmth of the sun on his face. He blinked in the early morning light and remembered what had happened the night before. He'd been warm. So fucking warm. Jules had curled herself around him and he'd slept like a baby.

He took a deep breath, loving everything about her scent. She smelled like citrus and sex. Shampoo and...well, him. He'd pretty well marked her the night before and he wasn't unhappy about that.

After he'd made love to her on the couch, he'd shifted them to the bedroom, candles and all because he'd been serious about being able to see her. He didn't want to miss a single look on her face. He loved how expressive she was. She gave it all away. Her eyes widened when he sucked on her nipples or slid a finger over her clit. She gasped and shuddered when he curled his long finger up inside her. Jules didn't hold back, and that was the sexiest thing he'd ever seen.

He rolled over and reached for her. This was how he wanted to start the morning. He would make love to her again and then they would plan the day. He had to meet with Chef, but other than that, he was hers all day long. He could meet with Chef and decide on the line assignments, and then maybe he would take his girl out for lunch and to the movies. Anything she wanted to see.

"Hey, baby," he started.

"Do you need coffee before you go?"

He sat up because that hadn't come from the other side of the bed. "What?"

Jules was standing at the end of the bed, a mug in her hand. It was obvious she'd been up for a while since it looked like she'd showered and dressed and done her hair. She wore gym clothes, but they somehow made her look all prim and proper, and that made him want to sex her up again.

Was she nervous? She hadn't had a relationship since her divorce and it didn't seem like her marriage had been hot in the sack. It was reasonable for her to be a little shy after a night of super-dirty sex. He needed to put her at ease, let her know it was okay to lounge around in bed with her lover. He gave her a smile. "You're up early, sweetheart. Why don't you come back to bed and when we're through, I'll make you some breakfast?"

"I already ate," she said, her tone brisk. She set the coffee on the nightstand. "I wasn't sure if you used cream and sugar, but they're both in the kitchen. I folded your clothes and they're ready for you on the dresser."

Whoa. What was happening? He took the coffee. "I like my coffee plain. This smells wonderful, but I kind of thought we would spend the morning together."

"I thought you spent Monday mornings with Chef."

Ah, that was the problem. She was trying to make things easy on him. That was sweet of her, but he didn't want easy. "He'll come by for a few minutes, but he won't stay for long. He'll eat breakfast if I have some made, otherwise he'll head home. He spends Mondays with Grace and the kids after he's worked out. It's no big deal."

"Well, I spend Monday mornings with Lance," she said with a nod. "And he gets cranky if I'm late."

Lance? Who the hell was Lance? "You've got a date?"

She shrugged. "Sure. If you call PT a date, then I've been dating

Lance for about six weeks. Then I've got a session with my shrink to make sure I'm handling life all right. It's all part of the lose-a-limb, work-at-Top package. I gotta get going. Busy day. You'll lock up on your way out?"

Lock up? He stood, going after her. "Jules, I thought we could spend some time together."

She grabbed her gym bag as she opened the door. "Like I said, busy day. But thank you for last night. I needed it." She glanced back inside, her eyes going wide. "Jeez, Leones. I told you where your pants were."

"If I'd taken the time to put my pants on, you would already have been gone." It wasn't like she hadn't seen everything anyway. He stood in the doorway because he was kind of worried if she left she might keep walking. He wasn't sure what the hell was happening. "We need to talk."

"Oh, dear." Mrs. Gleeson was standing next to Jules, holding the leash to her little yappy dog. "Javier, you seem to have lost your clothes."

Javier grabbed the raincoat Jules had hanging by the door. It managed to cover his junk.

She smiled up at him. "Or perhaps the whole place is going *au naturel*. I brought up the prospect at the last residents' meeting but that damn old man on four shut me down. You know clothes really do hide our truest selves. There's a beautiful community I go to sometimes in Colorado. You should come with me. You would love it there."

"You should put on some clothes," Jules insisted. "And there's nothing to talk about. We're cool. Now I have to walk Mrs. Gleeson down. Her daughter picks her up on Mondays and they go to lunch."

"Perhaps Laura can come here this time," Mrs. Gleeson offered. "After all, there's a show up here. And you know my Laura is divorced. She needs to start dating."

"Javier doesn't date," Jules explained, starting down the hall. She was really leaving.

What the hell had last night been? He thought about going after her. He could grab his pants. But he stood there staring as she walked down the hall.

"Morning, Chef," Jules said as she walked past Sean Taggart to get to the elevator.

"Morning, Jules."

Mrs. Gleeson lingered, watching Chef stride down the hall. He was pretty sure she was watching Taggart's butt.

Taggart stopped in the middle of the hallway. "I like the look, Javi. But that's not your apartment." Chef looked down the hallway where the elevator doors had closed and then back to Javi, one brow raised. "You and Jules?"

Javier couldn't remember the last time he felt so oddly exposed. Yes, he was standing there with a yellow latex rain slicker covering his willy, but the thing with him and Jules was new and apparently confusing. "The power went out."

"It apparently didn't go out of your dick," Chef said. "Jules got some coffee in there?"

"Yeah." She'd walked out on him. "She thanked me. What does that mean? She thanked me and told me to put on pants."

Chef stared at him for a moment. "No woman ever asked you to put on pants before?"

"They usually demand that I take them off."

"If you want me to talk to you about this, you're going to have to put on pants." Chef walked through and immediately found the coffee maker. "So this is seriously the first time you've ever had a woman walk out on you after you...you did spend the night, right?"

He grabbed his pants from the bedroom. He shouldn't talk about this. Sean Taggart was his boss. Sean didn't need to hear about his damn love life. "I came over because our power went out. I thought she might get scared."

Taggart had a mug in his hand and he was glancing around Jules's apartment with curious eyes. "You know she was in the Navy, right? You think a Navy vet gets scared of the dark."

But she had been. He could remember how soft his whole soul had gotten when he realized she was starting at every clap of thunder.

By the time he'd been done, she hadn't noticed the weather at all. "She lost her hand during a storm, or rather she began the process of losing it. I think the thunder bugs her."

"So you fucked her calm?"

"Hey, don't talk about her like that."

Chef stopped, looking him over. "I didn't mean any disrespect to Jules, Javi. Trust me. After a day of running after an overactive kid, taking care of a baby, and waiting to find out if her oldest is being deployed, I had to fuck Grace calm."

Yeah, and he would bet Grace hadn't told her husband to put on his pants and lock up when he left. "Sorry about that. What's on the menu for the week?"

Chef took a sip of coffee. "I emailed you the menu. I want to give Drake a shot at taking lead one night. I think Eric is going to lose his sous chef. Lodge is sniffing around. That club of his lost its executive chef. I want to start prepping Drake to move over to Fort Worth. The line chefs over there are good, but they're too green to take the secondary role. Are you sure you don't want to talk about it?"

Julian Lodge was a rival of Big Tag's, though Javier also thought they were somewhat friendly. When the two men got in the same room it was a little like two sharks circling, waiting to see if one would bite first or if they would both laugh and trade stories about their kills. It looked like Lodge was about to take a nibble.

The next softball game was going to be a ton of fun. Not that Lodge would play softball, but he would sit in the stands in his perfectly tailored suit and boo Big Tag.

"Of course I want to talk about the menus. It's my job." While Chef had been talking, he'd pulled up the menu. "Drake is great with duck. He can take the lead Thursday."

Chef was grinning. "He should be great with duck with a name like that, but I wasn't talking about the schedule and assignments. I was talking about what happened with you and Jules."

He was starting to think the thing with Jules hadn't gone as well as he'd thought it had, but he didn't want to burden his boss.

"Javi, who you going to talk to about this?" Chef asked. "Who would you normally talk to? Because you probably should talk about it or you could screw it up. Do you want this woman? I'll totally back off if this was one more hookup, but the look on your face as she walked away kind of told me it's not."

"I would talk to Rafe," he said quietly, missing his brother more in that moment than he had since the day he realized the brother he'd known was gone and might not come back.

"Can you talk to him?"

Javier shook his head. "No. When he's sober enough to listen, he's too bitter to do anything but spout crap about how his wife left him. I have no idea how Sonja held out for as long as she did. The last thing he's going to want to hear about is how I hooked up with a woman from work."

"Was that all it was?"

All he had to do was shrug and say yes and Sean would believe him. He would get back to the task at hand. And Javier would still be confused about what had happened. "No. I like her."

Sean shook his head approvingly. "She's a likable lady. She's only been in town for a few weeks and she's already volunteering to help out her fellow wounded vets. I like a person who throws herself into the community. You know she recently divorced."

"Not that recently." He didn't think she'd been mad in love with her ex.

"Still, I think it takes a while to get over something like that. Have you really honestly never had a woman turn you down?"

"Of course I have. Not lately. Though Kristy ran as fast as she possibly could."

"I heard you went back to your previous dating style after that didn't work out." Sean sat down at the kitchen table.

"Yeah," he admitted. "I went a little crazy for a week or two after Rafe showed up."

"You think that Jules didn't hear about it? Didn't see the women parading in and out or see you doing the walk of shame?"

"I couldn't leave Rafe. I had them over here." He sat down across from Sean, some of the words penetrating his brain. "You think she knew those women were there for sex?"

"Did they look like they were cleaning your apartment?"

In miniskirts and high heels? "Shit. She doesn't take me seriously. She thanked me."

A grin split Sean's face. "You're lucky she didn't slip you some cash and ask if you needed referrals."

The thought made him shudder. "Are you saying she used me for sex?"

"Wow, you sound like a prude for once. This is fun. I don't get to do this with my younger brothers anymore. They're all married and settled. My stepsons aren't even close to needing relationship advice. I didn't realize how long it's been since I had to walk some dipshit in my family through how to deal with a woman."

Javier put a hand on his chest. "Well, I should be your Disneyland then because I don't know what I did wrong. I showed up on her doorstep. I brought her wine. I was very careful with her. I even told her she wasn't like the other women."

"And she should believe you, why? That sounds like a great line to use."

"But it was true."

"How did you prepare her for this encounter?"

He wanted to go there? "Well, I gave her a starter orgasm first."

Sean held out a hand. "Not physically. How did you soften her up? Take her to dinner? Bring her some flowers just to brighten her day? Help her out at work?"

"I told you. I brought wine."

"You have never worked for a woman in your life, have you?"

"I work hard," Javier argued. "Do you know how fit you have to be to spend all night pleasuring a woman?"

"Do you know what it means to bounce a sleeping infant in your arms for four hours straight because if you don't keep the rhythm up he'll wake up and your wife is utterly exhausted?"

"No, but I don't have kids. I don't have a wife."

"And you never will if you think the only thing a woman needs from you is an orgasm. You have been playing around with party girls. Jules is an entirely different class of woman and no, she's not taking you seriously, but you haven't given her a reason to."

"I make sure I sit by her when we eat." Javier tried to defend himself, but he was starting to see Sean's point. "I make sure she gets to pick before Declan and Linc eat everything in sight. They're like locust."

"If you want her to believe she's different, treat her differently, and no, sleeping over doesn't count," Sean pointed out. "Getting your ass up before she wakes up and ensuring that she has coffee and a decent breakfast, well, that's a good start."

How had he gone so wrong? "I really like her."

"Good. Show her. Words are too easy. She needs to see that she's different."

"She thinks I'm a himbo."

"Almost certainly. And she's just come out of a relationship. She doesn't want to throw herself into another one that's almost certainly doomed to fail. She picked you as a nice transition from loneliness to finding her way back out into the world. When you think about it, she chose well. You're nice. You're good in bed. No one will blink if she sleeps with you and goes right back to being perfectly polite because that's what you do best."

"But I don't want that this time." It wasn't fair. Wow, he was thinking like a boy.

Sean patted his arm. "Then it's time to man up. You want this woman, you're going to have to work for her and you're going to have to be sneaky about it because I think she might get nervous if you come at her head-on."

Sneaky. He'd never had to be sneaky with a woman. "I need to find a way to spend time with her. And protect my virtue because I'm feeling a little used this morning. She tried to send me on my way with nothing but coffee. You would think she would have made me a muffin or something."

"I think spending time with her is definitely the key, and practicing a little virtue might not hurt." Sean put his hand on the small book that lay on the kitchen table. "But you also need to figure out what she needs that she won't talk about. This might be a good start."

"I think she was working on this when I showed up." He pulled the book into his hand and opened it. "Recipes. Wow. I bet these were her grandmother's. They're not elevated enough to be her mom's."

He flipped through the pages. He was a snob when it came to food, but there was something undeniably powerful about reading recipes that had been written out in a careful hand. It reminded him that he'd started cooking in his mother's kitchen, learning to make rice and beans because she'd gotten arthritis at an early age and when it flared up, he wanted to help her.

That was how he'd fallen in love with cooking. His mother's love had been in every dish, and when she couldn't cook anymore, he gave that love back to her.

Was this how Jules had gotten into cooking?

"So you know about her mom?" Sean asked.

"Yeah, Linc recognized her," he admitted, glancing at the notes she'd made. There were sticky notes on several of the recipes. Some of the notes made changes in ingredients while others shifted instructions, as though trying to make the recipe easier to cook somehow. "Any idea why she doesn't talk to her mom anymore? I asked her about her prosthetic. She's got a low-end model. She said it was all she could afford. Why wouldn't her mom help her out?"

"I get the feeling those are two stubborn women." Sean moved over so he could see the recipes, too. "I think she's trying to figure out how to make these dishes with one hand. The notes she's making are all about simplifying the steps."

"It's fine to simplify the steps, but she doesn't need to use pre-chopped onions. She can chop onions," Javier said. "She just needs practice."

"Says the man with two hands."

His brain was already working. He wanted her. He needed to figure out how to get her to take him seriously. Maybe Chef was right and he was going about this all wrong. He'd been looking at their differences, but they had a lot in common, too.

He'd been in the military. She'd been in the military. They both loved to cook. She'd lost the ability when she'd lost her hand, but she seemed to be trying to get back into it.

"I don't have to use them both." His mind was working. "I might have a plan, but it's going to require you to back me up."

"I got you," Sean promised. "If you really care about her, that is. If this is some kind of wounded masculine pride thing, reconsider. She's been through a lot."

"Which is precisely why she deserves the best." Now that he thought about it, this was better. She deserved to be pursued. If she just fell into his hands, he would never learn how to properly handle her. She wanted to run and hide? He could chase and find.

And the book in his hand might be exactly what he needed.

"Now let's go over the menu. I want to get home and spend the afternoon with my wife."

"Sure thing. Let me print it out," Javier said. "Come over to my place because I had some notes on the barbecue. And the special menu for the party coming up. How the hell did that happen anyway? I thought open mic night was a bust."

"That was when we let amateurs sing." Sean shook his head as he followed Javier out to the hall. "I thought it would be a good way to show off some of Dallas's untapped talent. Instead I got Jake singing "Babe" by Styx to Serena after four beers. The only good thing to come out of it was Ian taped the whole thing and now he plays it as the opening to every monthly conference. After that I shut it down, but it turns out Wade knows someone who knows an actual up-and-coming singer. I offered up the restaurant as a place she can kind of ease into. I think they like singers at her level to work the kinks out in smaller venues before they go to the larger ones. She's good. I listened to her album."

Javier locked the door behind him.

"Shouldn't you have put on your shirt?" Chef gave him his infamous judgey eye.

That's what Javier called it. Sean Taggart was excellent at conveying his disdain with that one brow. But in this case, it was all part of the plan. "I'm leaving it behind. I want to see if she brings it back to me or if she keeps it and sleeps in it."

Either way, he would have some information.

"See, now you're getting sneaky." There was approval in Sean's voice.

He meant to get much sneakier. She thought she could steal one night from him? She would find out exactly how different she was.

He strode to his apartment, getting his keys out of his pocket. He would get the assignments done and then maybe start to think about how to get his plan rolling.

"Javi, back up," Chef said suddenly.

That was when he realized he'd been reaching for the door, but it was already open, the handle slightly off from the frame.

"I locked it when I left." He glanced at Sean and felt his jaw drop. "Where did that come from?"

Chef was carrying a semiautomatic in his hand. "You feel comfortable without pants. I don't feel comfortable without a gun. Call Derek Brighton. Unless you left your phone behind, too."

His cell was in his pocket. It was good to know if a bunch of bad guys ever invaded Top, the executive chef remembered how to defend himself. Sean kicked the door open and stepped inside, every movement predatory.

Luckily, he had Derek Brighton's number programmed into his phone. Lieutenant Brighton was a friend of the Taggarts and the go-to guy on the DPD when they needed some law enforcement.

Sean stepped back out. "You must have pissed someone off mightily. It's safe to go in but try not to touch anything. I'll talk to Derek."

He passed the phone to Sean and walked through the door. Someone had trashed the place. It looked like every piece of furniture he owned had been overturned and left there like a used and discarded toy.

What the hell? Who would want to hurt him like this?

"Brighton's on his way. He'll see what we can get from security cameras. You have insurance?" The gun seemed to have disappeared and Javier wondered where the holster was.

He felt sick to his stomach. Chaos. It was pure chaos.

"Yeah. I'll find the policy. I've got it in a safe Dec installed for me."

"You want me to call Ian? He can have someone out here in under an hour," Sean promised.

"Nah. I would bet it was some punk kids who took advantage of the storm." He winced. "Which likely knocked out the security cameras. Damn, I wonder how many of us got hit last night."

He breathed a little easier because that made sense. This was the city. Things got stolen. People took advantage.

"Let's try to knock this out while we're waiting for Derek. You'll still need a police report. How do you feel about ceviche?" Chef pulled the couch back into its proper position.

At least the assholes hadn't taken a knife to it. It looked like they'd come in and turned everything over looking for cash or valuables.

It wasn't personal.

But his ceviche was. "I feel good about it, boss."

He would clean the place up and then start in on his plan.

Because he was getting the girl this time. He would make sure of it.

* * * *

"So you started an affair last night? With a coworker?" Kai Ferguson studied her, looking over his glasses, his notebook in hand. "How did that make you feel?"

How had she felt when Javier had kissed her? When he'd smiled that crazy sexy smile of his and touched her like he couldn't stop? How had she felt when she'd put her head on his chest, utterly exhausted, and slept despite the ferocity of the storm outside?

"I feel good about it," she replied. She wasn't sure why she'd told her therapist about Javier. Kai had a way of getting people to open up around him. It was probably why he'd gone into shrinkdom. But she had to clear up a few misconceptions. "But it's not an affair. It was just a one-night thing."

"Ah," Kai said. "So it just happened organically? Or you talked about it?"

"There wasn't a lot of talking involved, Doc." Just a lot of righteously amazing sex and then she'd slept like a baby. No bad dreams. No waking up and reaching out with her left hand for the bottle of water she kept on the side table because just for a second she forgot. She'd slept with her head on his chest and it had been hard to leave him there.

She'd thought about kissing him awake and seeing if he maybe wanted her to cook some breakfast for them.

Then she'd remembered that he was a chef. Not just any chef. He was the sous chef to a man who would likely have a Michelin star under his belt if he worked in New York. Javier Leones was going places. One day he'd open a third Top or he'd go off on his own. As gorgeous as he was, he might get his own TV show like her mom, and then she'd be right back where she'd started.

And all she could really offer him was some toast. Which he would have to butter himself.

She'd rolled out of bed as cautiously as she could, not wanting to wake him.

"How do you know what your partner wants if you don't talk to him?" Kai asked. "I think it's a mistake to go into any kind of a relationship without some sort of negotiation."

"I'm pretty sure he wanted sex." She'd opened the door. She might as well walk through it. In the months since she'd moved to Dallas, she'd come to find these sessions with Kai soothing. It was good to talk, and she didn't have to worry about him blabbing to anyone else. She'd found herself opening up more and more to the good doc and using these sessions as a way to make decisions. Well, she definitely had a decision to make and it would be better with Kai's input. "This is Javier we're talking about."

"Oh." A knowing grin crossed Kai's face. "I thought we were talking about someone else."

"Who?" She was curious.

He shrugged a little. "I don't know. One of the line chefs perhaps. Someone you have more in common with."

"I have lots in common with Javier. He's pretty chill and easy to talk to. We both come from military backgrounds. He's dealing with a brother who's going through the transition of losing a couple of limbs."

"You both grew up working in kitchens," Kai said quietly. "I happen to know that all of his teenage jobs were in kitchens. When his family got in trouble, he lied about his age and got a job washing dishes. He was fourteen. He managed school and working until almost midnight five nights a week. You worked for your mom in the beginning, didn't you?"

It was always hard to think about her mom. Especially those early years when they'd only had each other. "I helped her can her jams and jellies. I would come home from school and she would be exhausted so I would do what I could to give her a break."

"Yes, I can see you do have a lot in common with Javier." It was said with a small note of satisfaction, as though she'd fallen into a well-planned trap and he'd known all along who they'd been talking about.

"Should you be talking about Javier to me? About his private stuff?" It made her nervous that Kai wasn't as careful as she thought he would be.

"Javier isn't a patient. He's a friend and he's not quiet about his past. I'm not telling you anything he wouldn't tell you if you'd taken the time to talk to him."

She didn't like how that sounded. "I've talked to him. We work together. It's not like I invited some random dude into bed with me."

Kai held a hand up. "I'm not judging you, Jules. I'm happy you've taken a step to get back into life. You've told me how you feel like time stopped and you're not moving forward."

She felt like she was trapped, like she was stuck in a river and it rushed all around her, but she was immovable. Caught in one place while the world rushed by her. "Yeah. I still feel like that sometimes.

I'm trying to adapt."

"Are you?"

Was he high? "Yeah. I think getting back out in the world and getting a job and trying to move on is kind of the definition of adaptation."

He was quiet for a moment. That was when she always felt the most awkward. "What was your dream? Before the accident?"

She went silent, wishing she hadn't mentioned anything at all. He'd made her comfortable all these weeks and now she was paying the price. They'd talked about the past, a bit about her plans for the future, but this was starting to feel heavy.

Still, she'd promised herself when she started this that she would attempt to make a go of it. She wasn't sure she believed that therapy could make her a better person, but so far it hadn't hurt her either. "I don't know."

"What was your dream when you were a kid?" he asked.

"The usual. I went through a marine biology phase. I liked dolphins. I wanted to be an astronaut for a while."

"There wasn't any one thing you were truly interested in?"

She shrugged. "I liked to cook. I was kind of around it a lot."

"Yes, I can imagine with your mother's business. Did she teach you?"

"In the beginning," Jules said cautiously. "When my dad was around, she was a housewife and I was the only kid. She taught me how to bake and I would hang out with her when she made dinner. She told me food was the way to a man's heart. Guess my dad didn't have a heart."

"How old were you when he divorced your mom?"

"I was eight. And it wasn't like other divorces I saw. There was no shuffling me around and fighting over who got what time with me. My dad full on left and didn't look back. He got his divorce and didn't want any custody. He moved to Montana with his secretary. I think they've got a couple of kids now, but I've never met them."

"That kind of desertion can be hard on a kid."

"You're telling me."

"Hard on your mom, too," he said quietly. "Tell me something— did you plan on staying in the military? Were you going to make a career out of it? I would think given your mother's success that you might have followed in her footsteps."

Those footsteps had been big and impossible to fill. She hadn't even wanted to try. That lifestyle wasn't for her. She'd hated the cameras and the scrutiny and always having to look perfect. "I went into the Navy because I needed something different. Do you know what it's like to go from working hard every day and having nothing to being mommy's pampered princess?"

"Sounds like a First World problem to me."

He had a point. "It wasn't that I hated finally having money. I liked that my mom wasn't worried about losing the house. But what I couldn't make her understand was that it was her accomplishment. Not mine. I hated all the crap that went with her job. Producers, publicists. It was too much and it made me feel empty. Hell, she doesn't even do her own cooking anymore. She's got test kitchens."

I don't want you in there, baby girl. I want you with me. Running the business is where you make the money. We're never going to be in a position again where we have to cook for a living.

But that had been exactly what Jules had wanted to do.

Kai sat up. "Yes, I'd heard that's how some of those big machines work. I know your mother is a woman, but her business runs like a well-oiled machine. If you worked with her when you were a kid, why didn't she give you a place in the business?"

Yes, her place in the business had been the problem. "She did. She told me I could go to college and get a business degree and she would eventually make me the CEO of the company."

"That's an impressive offer."

"I hate the business side, Doc," Jules admitted. "She made me go to business meetings as a teenager and I couldn't keep my eyes open. The one job I wanted she told me was beneath me."

"The test kitchens," he surmised. "You wanted to run them."

Well, no one said he was stupid. "Yeah. I thought one of us should. I didn't ask to run them in the beginning. I just wanted to work there. Food is…it's meaningful."

"It certainly is to a chef. Your mother started out as a Southern cook?"

Jules nodded. "She was a home cook. My grandma taught her, but Mom wanted more. After she sold her jam recipe to a big conglomerate, they made her the face of that division. She was beautiful and charming and she kind of skyrocketed from there."

"And left you behind?"

"Of course not. She took me with her. She wasn't some monster."

Kai's lips quirked up. "I wasn't speaking in a literal fashion. I mean she left the little girl who helped her mother make jam behind. She needed a princess for her palace and you weren't that girl."

Wow. That was hitting the nail on the head. How had he seen so much from the little she'd told him? "Yes. You get it. That's why it was hard and that's why I left. I met Kevin in my first year of college. I hated every class I went to. I wanted a job. I wanted to cook, but my mother insisted she knew best. She was very controlling. She used that money she made like a weapon. Kevin's father was the same way. Wanted him to be a lawyer and nothing else would do. So we made the choice."

"To tell your parents to go to hell?"

It had been about more than rebellion. "And to grab some freedom for ourselves. I know it sounds like I was some poor little rich girl, but I found that life oppressive. I honestly liked the Navy. I felt like I was doing something good. Like I was making a difference. My mom tells people what kind of pillows to buy. It felt empty to me. Do you know where I spent half my off-duty time on the ships I was assigned to?"

"I can bet," Kai replied. "Did they let you in the kitchens?"

She smiled at the memory. "Yeah, it was the first time I'd been able to learn in forever. The cook was an older guy who'd been in the service for years. He'd been just about everywhere and he was happy to teach me. I miss that old man."

"Do you keep in touch?"

Hank. How long had it been? He'd come to see her in the hospital after the accident, but once she'd come home she'd talked to almost no one. "Nah, he's still on a boat. And all we talked about was food. I don't cook anymore so…"

Kai nodded her way. "And that is why I question your use of the word adapting."

"What do you mean?"

He adjusted his glasses. "Adaptation means you shift. You find new ways to make a thing suitable to a purpose. How have you adapted, Jules?"

She shifted in her chair, the turn of the conversation suddenly making her uncomfortable. "Well, I figured out how to type with one hand. I suck at it, but I can manage an email."

"And your dream job is to be an admin?"

"Of course not."

"Then how is typing going to help you achieve the goal?" His questions came quickly now, as though he'd found the right line of investigation and he wasn't about to let up.

"Who said I have a goal?"

"You can sit here and tell me you didn't have a particular dream, but I call bullshit on that. You wanted to cook. You wanted to be a chef."

"I was a kid then," she said. "I'm an adult now. And I don't have a goal except to get through this day and move on to the next."

He stopped for a moment and she could practically feel his disappointment. "Then you're not adapting, Jules. You're merely surviving."

She felt her hand fist in her lap. "Why are you on my case?"

"Because I think you've gotten complacent." His tone was back to soothing, but she couldn't ignore the words. They didn't soothe at all. "I think if no one pushes you, in a few years, you'll still be exactly where you are right now. Maybe you'll move on to another job, but it won't be the one you want."

He didn't understand. She'd known when she'd gotten the news from the doctor that they were amputating her hand that she wasn't going to work in a restaurant. Not the way she'd envisioned. "I can't cook at the level I wanted to. Isn't it better to accept that and move on with my life?"

"Or you could fight like hell to get what you want. There's a reason you came here. To Dallas, to work at Top. You surrounded yourself with people who had to fight their way back. That can be motivating. Let them help you. There is very little in this life that you can't do with some adaptation and a shitload of hard work, Jules. And maybe that includes understanding that you don't know what other people are thinking."

"What is that supposed to mean?"

"It means we don't always understand other people's motivations. We filter their reactions through our own experiences and that leads to misunderstandings," he explained. "It means you have no idea why Javier slept with you last night. Did he say it was only for one night?"

She rolled her eyes because he was being naïve. "It's implied because he's Javier."

"Who you've spent a lot of time with and you can read his mind."

"I say that because I watch the women come in and out of his apartment, and I'm pretty sure they're not housekeepers or nursing his brother. No man who goes through that many women is looking for some kind of relationship."

"You're not willing to give him a chance?"

Frustration welled inside her. "There's no chance to be given. Look, Doc, I get that you think I'm in some kind of limbo, but I'm trying. I'm the kind of woman who doesn't want to even attempt to do something if I can't give it my all. I'm never going to cook at the level Chef is. I'm not suited to even be a line chef at Top. I can't cut veg for salads. But that doesn't mean I don't have projects. I'm playing around with some of my grandmother's old recipes, trying to see if I can adapt them for what I can do."

"How do you know what you can do if you don't try?"

She stood up, unable to stay still a second longer. "You think I haven't? I don't even have my dominant hand. Do you know how sharp a chef's knife is?"

She had the scars from trying. She'd cut herself a couple of times and what she'd managed to do to those vegetables should be a crime. It had been terrible, worse than any amateur.

He held a hand up, signaling his willingness to end the discussion. "I'll take your word on it. I'm sorry. It's part of my job to try to make you see things from another point of view."

"There's not another point of view about this. There's me and what I can do now that I'm here. If that's not good enough for you, then I don't know what else to do." She didn't want to lose her job, but she wasn't sure what else to say. "I do rehab twice a week. I volunteer to help people in my position. Hell, I help out at PT with other patients."

"Jules, don't think I don't understand how willing you are to help a friend, a stranger even. I wasn't talking about that. You're good at your job. You're disciplined and kind. You would move mountains to help a friend, but you have to love yourself, too. You have to love yourself enough to give you a chance."

She stared at him for a moment. "I don't know what you want from me, Doc."

He stood up and laid aside the notepad he'd been holding. "How about we make a deal? You try one thing that scares you this week. I don't care what it is. It could be anything from bungee jumping to touching a spider. It doesn't matter. Say yes to one thing that scares you and next week, we'll talk about whatever you want to talk about. Hell, we'll play Xbox if you want and that can count as therapy for the week."

Because her job at Top required these sessions, required her PT. She understood it. Taggart hired broken things and needed to make sure they were willing to try to put themselves back together again. Committing to PT and sessions with Kai proved the employee was dedicated to getting better, being better.

One thing that scared her. She hated clowns. She could force herself to find a clown and not kill it. She'd already figured out how to handle thunderstorms. She wasn't thrilled with heights. Maybe she could try taking a tour of one of the high-rises around Dallas.

Or she could do the thing that scared her and also intrigued her.

"I'll go to the play party."

She was kind of cheating. She'd made this decision shortly after waking up next to Javier. But she wasn't lying. It did scare her. The idea of people looking at her, being so exposed… It scared her and made her wonder.

Kai's smile lit up his handsome face. "Excellent. I think that's a perfect thing to do. Does that decision have anything to do with last night?"

Well, she wasn't fooling the doc. "Yes. I guess Javier showed me that I could move on in this area of my life, too. Maybe you're right about that. I have been stuck when it comes to reaching out to other people. Maybe I've been stuck for longer than you would suspect. My marriage wasn't great even before the accident. I fell into it because we seemed to want the same things."

"Does the intimacy scare you?"

She thought about it for a moment. "What scares me the most is that I know if I think about it for too long, the glow from last night will wear off and all my insecurities will come back. Javier made me feel like I was beautiful. I thank him for that. But last night was a one-off. How long will it be before I go back to questioning every moment of the encounter and whether or not I really need physical touch and affection? If I let it go too long, I'll decide I'm an intellectual creature who can survive without anyone or some shit. I liked being touched. It made me feel alive in a way I haven't in a very long time."

She needed to try again. She'd been in her hole for eighteen months and it was time to pull herself together and start life over.

Without her husband or the job she'd loved. Without her mother. Without her hand.

Kai touched her shoulder. "I'll find a good mentor for you. You'll be there to observe, but if you decide you want to try something, talk to your mentor and he or she will facilitate the encounter."

"He or she?"

"Unless you have a preference."

"You told me I should do what scares me, right? Get me a Dom, Doc. In for a penny and all." A Dom. A man who would be there to protect her and teach her and help her decide if this was something she wanted to explore. It would bring her more fully into the world her coworkers lived in. She would be going to a party at her ex-husband's friend's house.

It was weird. She got butterflies thinking about it

Would Javier be there? Would he have a new gorgeous woman at his side?

If he did, she would smile and high-five him.

Well, maybe not high-five him, but she wouldn't act like the world had ended. She wasn't going to be some clinging vine, nor would she hold last night against him. When she saw him in the hallway or at Top, they would go on the way they had.

Like he'd never kissed her as if she was the only woman on the planet. Like she hadn't wrapped herself around him and held on for dear life.

She would be his friend and always thank him for waking up this side of her.

"A Dom it is then. I'll think about it and select someone you'll match well with." He reached out and took her hand in his. "This is good. I know you're annoyed with me, but sometimes that's the sign of the start of a breakthrough," Kai explained. "I'll let Kori know you're going. You can ride out with us if you like. And she'll be more than happy to help you find some fet wear."

"Fet wear?" She hadn't thought about fet wear.

"Yes, no street clothes allowed," he said with a wink. "Kori can explain it all to you. She lives to shop. Well, for anything kinky or anything for our dogs. Otherwise she complains about shopping. You'll be making my wife very happy. Sometimes I'm not sure if what she's bought is for herself or the dogs until she tells me."

Fet wear. Kinky stuff. She took a deep breath. "Sounds good. And I'll take you up on the Xbox next week."

"Absolutely." He let her hand go and started to walk toward the door.

Somehow she had a feeling the doc would find a way to turn killing aliens into some kind of life lesson because even as he was joking with his wife about taking Jules shopping, her brain was working.

Was there another point of view? Was she giving up too fast, accepting what life offered her without fighting for what she wanted?

She stopped at Kori's desk and told the other woman what she needed. The doctor's wife was more than pleased to accommodate her.

Jules walked out of the building, letting the sun hit her face.

She couldn't help but wonder if Javier was enjoying the day.

Would she cross paths with him in the hallway? She wasn't sure how to act. She needed an etiquette book. Did she say thanks again? Did she praise him for his incredible prowess in the bedroom?

Jules took a deep breath. She would handle it when it came up. After all, how hard could it be?

Chapter Four

Javier crossed his arms over his chest and frowned. "Excuse me? What did you just say?"

Eric Vail set down the box he'd carried in. "I asked if you were giving Jules a ride to the party. I figured you might come together since you're in the same building. No? You can certainly take two cars. No one's going to check your carbon footprint at the door. I was asking because I kind of thought you two were friends."

Friends? He'd thought they were friends, too, but friends didn't use each other for sex and then avoid their friendly sex partner like he had the plague. The one time in the last few days he'd managed to catch her, she'd been polite. She'd asked about his day, told him she'd been to a session with her therapist. When he'd asked if she would join him for dinner, she'd turned a perfect shade of pink and mumbled something about having plans and disappeared into her apartment.

It rankled. It also made him more certain than ever that they needed to talk, and unless she was going to quit her job, that talk was coming faster than she thought.

"I was unaware that Jules had decided to join us." He hadn't planned to go, either, but only because he couldn't work up the will to play. He'd been about to tell Eric he was staying home. Between Rafe getting out the hospital and the fact that he didn't want some random play partner, he'd convinced himself to stay in. He'd decided he would ask Jules if she wanted to catch a late movie with him, put their relationship back on the right track.

Chef had been correct. He'd thought about what had gone wrong for days. He had to show her she was different, and that meant a two-pronged assault on her senses. He had work Javier and fun Javier.

And now he had pissed-off Javier because she was going to a play party without him.

They definitely needed to have a talk.

"Who's walking her around?" There was no question that she would be coming alone. Even though this was a private party, she was a tourist and would need someone to be responsible for her.

"Kai matched her with one of my line chefs. His name is Cal. Good guy," Eric replied.

"Does he like his life? Because if he lays a hand on her, I'll make sure it all goes to hell."

Eric stopped, staring at him for a moment. "Holy shit."

Chef stepped up and put a hand on Javi's shoulder. "Is your girl trying to get away? I heard from Kai that she's going to the party. I meant to ask if she was your date."

"Nope. Apparently, she's going with Cal, who will soon find out that he's not needed for the evening." This was what jealousy felt like. He didn't like it. The thought of Jules being led around by big, strong ex-football playing Cal was one he liked even less. "Except Cal is going to be conveniently unavailable to aid her in this."

"Nice play," Chef said approvingly. "I suspect you have someone else in mind."

"It's going to be me or no one at all."

Eric watched them like he couldn't quite understand the conversation. "When did Javier get all caveman about a woman?"

"When he met the right one," Chef said with a smile.

Eric shook his head. "You poor bastard. You finally meet a woman you want more than a night with and she's giving you hell?"

"She's being difficult," Javier allowed. "But I think it's because she's afraid. I'm going to try something when she gets in tonight. If it doesn't work I'll back off. I'm not some asshole who thinks a woman should fall in line because I want her to. If she's not into me, I'll let Cal escort her and I'll be polite as hell. I like her. I don't mean to grind her down if she can't care about me the way I care about her."

"Who are you and what did you do with Javi?" Eric looked at Sean. "He's a pod person, Chef. We've gotta get the real one back."

He flipped Eric the bird. "I'm not an asshole."

Sean chuckled. "He's closing up his manwhore shop. You know we all do it when the right one comes along. Although he does seem to have trouble corralling her. I would be concerned, but I think Javi's right. She's scared of his reputation. I know she's interested in him. I've seen how she watches him."

"And she didn't bring back my shirt." That had given him some hope.

"Wow. You're telling me you slept with her and you're now trying to get her to go out with you?" Eric asked. "Miracles happen. This is going to be an interesting play party. I'll make sure to tell Cal that you intend to beat the shit out of him for offering to politely escort your non-girlfriend around."

Fine. He was being an ass about Cal. "Or you could ask him if he wouldn't mind helping a brother out. A brother who can't get a woman out of his head. I would be eternally grateful if he would give me this chance with her. And I'll talk to Kai, too. But only if she responds to our talk the way I think she will."

"And if she doesn't?" Eric asked.

His stomach clenched at the thought. "Then I'll step back and leave her be and only execute part of my plan. The work part."

Eric put a hand on the box he'd brought with him. "Ah, this is for her. I wondered why you had me pick it up. I thought she was a hostess."

"No," Javier said with resolve. He'd read the notes she'd made in her grandmother's cookbook. She was trying, but he thought she was going about it the wrong way. She was trying to simplify the recipes she adored when she needed to train herself how to cook again. "She's a chef, or she wants to be. She tweaks recipes all the time."

"She does always have something to say and doesn't mind saying it," Chef admitted. "And she's usually right. I'm with Javi. She's a chef, but she doesn't think she can do it. She's holding herself back and everyone's treating her like a victim and not what she is."

"A survivor and a soldier," Javier finished. He'd thought about it for days. It was where he was going wrong with Rafe. He needed to be tough with his brother. Soft hadn't worked. Soft had left Rafe a whining needy mess. Starting when Rafe came home, he would get different treatment. "Let's see it. I want it out in the open when she comes in."

Eric opened the box and pulled out the custom-made cutting board. It had several different groupings of thin nails sticking up from the surface, perfect for holding whatever she would need to cut in place. She would be able to move the veg easily and clean up in minutes.

"It was the only one in Texas," Chef said. "We're lucky it was in Fort Worth."

"It's perfect. I'm going to play around with it. I want to know how hard it is." Javier meant to practice in case she wanted help. Otherwise, he was going to let it sit for a day or two and then start his plan. "Luckily, I'm surrounded by dudes who can tie a hand down."

Eric grinned. "Yeah, I think that won't be a problem." He sobered slightly. "This is a lot of trouble to go through for a woman. You're planning on doing this even if she doesn't want you?"

"Her wanting me or not doesn't change how I feel about her." Hell, doing this might make her hate him. It might not work. What did he know about getting stubborn women to come to their senses? He'd been looking through the Internet at videos showing how to use a knife with one hand. How to cook with one hand.

She'd helped him, tried to help Rafe. How could he not do the same for her?

Eric reached over and selected an onion from the basket they had. He held it out. "Then you're ready. I'll make sure Cal understands.

Let's give it a try."

He glanced up at the clock. He had about three hours before she showed up. That would give him practice time. He held up his left hand. "Let's tie this sucker down."

Chef already had rope in his hand. He was always prepared. "Nope. Other hand. She's doing this with her non-dominant hand. We will, too."

Damn. He put his right hand behind his back. This was going to be rough.

But worth it if it got him the girl.

* * * *

Jules stepped out of the locker room and nearly walked straight into Ally. She gasped and jumped back, her arm knocking against the door.

Ally's eyes went wide and she reached out. "I'm sorry. I didn't mean to startle you. Are you okay?"

Jules held up her prosthetic. "This one's hard to hurt. I'm good."

As good as she could be when she was kind of a mess. She'd screwed up with Javier. He'd been nice and polite and she'd practically run the other way. It was the invitation that had gotten to her. She'd had a smile on her face the rest of the time, trying to settle into being cool around the guy who'd blown her mind. She'd been ready for him to ask her to keep their night together on the down low. Sure, she was going to say. Wouldn't have it any other way.

He'd asked if she wanted to spend the evening with him.

That was when she'd run and hid and felt like a moron because she'd found his shirt and she'd slept in it. Who left his shirt behind? Had he just walked around all day without a shirt on? That would have been really nice to see. She could be down with that.

Dumbass. She was such a dumbass.

Ally gave her a smile. "Sorry. I was coming to find you. You're wanted in Chef's office."

That sounded bad. Chef barely spoke to her. She got all her

orders from Grace, who ran the front of house and generally kept things moving smoothly while her husband ran the kitchen. "Okay. Now? I haven't updated the menus yet."

"He said now." Ally's look changed to obvious sympathy. "I wouldn't make him wait. He's in a mood. Never quite seen him that serious."

Was she about to lose her job? Because she'd slept with Javi? Now that she thought about it, the waitresses he'd slept with were all gone. She didn't think they got fired, and they hadn't left right after they'd spent the night with the sous chef, but they were gone.

Because it was way easier to find a hostess than a talented chef. She was expendable and Javier wasn't. But she hadn't been planning on causing trouble. Why should she get fired?

She looked at the door and then back to the kitchen.

Maybe she should have taken him up on that dinner invitation. Maybe if she'd slept with him again, she might have gotten a couple more weeks of employment out of it.

Did Javier think she was going to make this easy on him? Did he think she would go into Sean Taggart's office and let Chef do the dirty work for him? If she'd become inconvenient to Javier, then she would show him exactly how fucking inconvenient she could be.

"Uh, Jules, that's not the way to the office," Ally said, sounding uncertain.

"That's because I'm not talking to Chef." Anger thrummed through her system. She didn't do this. She wasn't this crazy-ass bitch. When her husband had told her he wanted a divorce, she'd nodded and then they'd calmly made plans to find a lawyer and get it done.

So why did she suddenly want to pick up a baseball bat and let Javier know he couldn't get rid of her without a fight?

She shoved through the double doors that led to the kitchen, her blood pounding through her body. It kind of felt good. Like she'd been sleeping for a long time and now she was vibrantly awake. She would sue them all. She would take the place down.

It was a little like what she'd felt the other night in Javier's arms.

Awake and alive.

And angry. Super fucking angry.

"Javier!" She shouted his name because he needed to know that she was coming and she wasn't going quietly into Chef's office to let some other man handle their business. "Get out here, you fucking coward."

Mark, one of the line chefs, looked up from where he'd been seasoning the short ribs. "Uh, Jules, you okay?"

"I will be once one of you hauls Javier out here for me." Where the hell was he hiding? "If he thinks I'm going to slink away like one of his pathetic, no-last-name hookups, he needs to think again. And if he's been talking locker room shit about me with you guys, well, you're just as bad as him."

All of their eyes were on her. The kitchen always hummed with activity, but now it was perfectly silent because no one was interested in anything except the crazy lady in their midst.

Macon seemed to have stopped mid ice. He held a pastry bag in his hand, several delicate-looking cakes in various states of decoration. "Jules, should I call Kai?"

Because everyone here shared a damn therapist. She would lose her therapist and her job and she would have to find new friends. It wasn't fair and she'd realized how uncool she was with not fucking fair. Her life hadn't been fair. Had it been fair that she lost her hand and her husband and her dreams? Was it fair her mom had chosen her career over her daughter?

So one damn thing could be fair.

"Why would you call Kai, Macon? Because I'm upset? Because a woman gets angry that she's not being treated with some form of kindness? Does that make me crazy? Because I don't feel crazy. I feel pissed and I'm pissed at Javier. But I could be pissed at you. Do you want me to be pissed at you, Macon?"

Macon's eyes went wide. "No, ma'am."

Declan Burke was leaning against one of the prep tables. The big bodyguard had been hanging around for weeks prepping for the show coming up soon. "See, now that's crazy eyes. If anyone has not seen them before, that's what they look like. Javier's in trouble."

She was sick of this. "Where is he?"

A familiar form peeled away from the shadows at the back of the kitchen. "Well, last I heard, he was hanging out in my office hoping to talk to you."

Jules went still and felt her whole body become one big old embarrassed flame. She had to be bright red because Chef Taggart was standing in front of her, an amused expression on his face. "I thought you were in your office."

He wiped his hands dry with a dishcloth and shoved it back into the pocket of the knee-length apron he wore. "Nope. We don't have anything to talk about. Unless there's something I don't know about. Has Javier been doing something he shouldn't? Has he been harassing you?"

She shook her head quickly. She wasn't sure what was happening, but she'd obviously made an enormous mistake. "No, sir. Not at all. He's very nice to me. Uhm, I was playing a joke on him. You know how sometimes crazy women show up and want to yell at Javier."

Chef couldn't quite hide his amusement. "No. That hasn't happened often."

"Sometimes women at nightclubs slap him because he forgets he already met them and tries to hook up with them again," Macon allowed.

"That hasn't happened in forever," a familiar voice said.

She turned and Javier was standing in the doorway, a concerned look on his face.

"Let's give them a moment," Chef said. "Make it fast, you two. Those ribs won't braise themselves."

She watched as one by one the men strode out of the kitchen. Javier was standing by the doors, his arms crossed over his black chef jacket. Something about him in that uniform did it for her, but he was staring at her like she'd grown two heads.

And she kind of had. What had she been thinking? She wasn't the girl who lost it like that.

"Juliana, I asked to speak with you in the office. Is there a reason you were looking for me in here?"

Wow, she'd never heard him sound so serious unless he was yelling at the line chefs for burning a sauce or something. Javier always sounded like he was having a good time. Not now. His voice had gone dark and deep and she didn't like the fact that the impulse was right there to walk up to him and try to soothe him. That wasn't her place. She needed to tell him the truth. They would laugh about what a lunatic she was and move on. It was the only way out of this.

"I'm sorry. I thought Chef wanted to talk to me." Ally hadn't mentioned it was Javier. She'd merely told Jules she was wanted in the office.

"Why would Chef want to talk to you?"

She tried to smile, to brush the whole thing off. "Honestly, this is the craziest thing, Javier. For a minute, I thought he was going to fire me."

Javier's face went blank, as though he was trying to figure out what she meant, and then a look passed there that could only be described as pain. His eyes closed and when he opened them he looked deeply disappointed. "You thought I asked Chef to fire you? That's why you came looking for me. You were angry because I was going to have you dismissed. Tell me something, Juliana. Was I doing it because we slept together and I'm the bastard who doesn't want to deal with a woman I've already had? Or because I'm the bastard who can't handle a woman rejecting him?"

Her stomach did a deep dive because never in a million years had she thought he would be hurt. He was a good-time guy. He laughed everything off. "I know you slept with a couple of other people from the front of house and they're gone. It was stupid, but it was the first thing that crossed my mind."

Because deep down she'd known something bad would happen. It had to because it had felt good to be with him. Something had to be wrong.

"Jen left because she went back to college. Melinda took a job in Fort Worth after she met her fiancé. I introduced them, by the way.

They were lovely women. Why would I hurt them?" He straightened up, as though steeling himself. "I called you into the office because I wanted you to know that I would act professionally around you here at work, but I needed to ask you why you blew me off last night. I thought it was because you didn't understand that I meant what I said that night we spent together. You're different. I want to spend time with you. I want to try with you. That's what I meant to say. But I suspect that wouldn't have gone well for me."

This was what mortification felt like. He wanted to try with her? Try a relationship with him? With a big gorgeous god of a man who could cook? "I'm sorry. I didn't realize you felt that way."

He shook his head. "But I told you how I felt. We talked about it that night. I told you how different you were."

But they hadn't talked about it. He'd said things and she'd jumped to conclusions because she'd known she couldn't believe him. All of Kai's words were coming back to haunt her. They hadn't talked at all. They hadn't told each other what they wanted or needed because she'd thought it was merely a good time.

"I thought that was a line. The part about me being different. I figured you told every woman that." How could this be happening? Every word that came out of her mouth damned her further. "If it helps I thought it was a good line."

He laughed but it was a bitter sound. "No. That doesn't help. Let's go over who I am in your head. I'm a player who'll say anything to get in a woman's bed, and after I'm there I get rid of them so I...what? Don't have to look at them anymore? Or am I trying to bring in some piece of ass I can use? Which one is it, Jules?"

"I didn't say that. Not that way." But she'd thought it. Deep down, she'd thought it even as he was being nice to her. She'd thought that the only reason a man as gorgeous as him would want her is because he'd fuck anyone.

She needed way more therapy.

He moved closer to her and it took everything she had not to back up. "What way did you say it then?"

She forced herself to look into his eyes. He was so close now she could feel the heat coming off of him. "I didn't say anything. I was upset. I will admit that I obviously didn't think our encounter was what you think it was. We weren't on the same page."

"Our encounter? I made love to you. Three times that night. I worshipped your body and you call it an encounter?"

She couldn't look at him. He was too gorgeous, too upset with her. She glanced down at his chest. Even though she knew she should walk away, she couldn't seem to find the will. She'd made an idiot of herself over this man and she wanted a few answers. "What would you call it?"

"Life changing, but I'm obviously the only one." He reached out and brought her chin up. "So that was nothing but a random hookup for you?"

"I told you I don't like storms. I needed a distraction."

"So you would have slept with anyone who had knocked on your door?" Javier asked.

"Of course not. I wouldn't have slept with anyone but you. I knew it wouldn't mean anything with you."

"Except it *did* mean something to me." He stepped back. "So you used me as some kind of distraction."

That sounded utterly ridiculous. "Damn it, Javier. Don't act like some shrinking virgin who just had his innocence stolen. How many women have you slept with?"

He threw his hands up, his irritation obvious. "Why should that matter? All of that was before I met you. All that should matter now is how I act around you, how I treat you. I get it. I fucked up. I wanted you and I was so eager to have you I didn't think for a single second that you didn't want me the same way."

"I did want you." She couldn't argue with that. She still wanted him. Desperately. She thought about him constantly, but she knew it wouldn't work.

"You wanted me for sex," he corrected. "I wanted you. All of you."

"You don't know me."

He stared at her for a moment. "I don't know you? I know way more than you think I do. I know you're more self-conscious about that arm than you want anyone to see. I know there's zero reason to be because you're amazing and kind and smart. You help the people around you even when they don't deserve it. You like classic rock. You dance a little when it comes on before or after hours. You love to cook, but you don't do it anymore. That doesn't stop you from telling everyone else how to do it though because your mind is always working, always thinking about the dish. It's why you chose to work in a restaurant. You can't stay away from it."

How had he seen so much? She hadn't realized he was watching her at all. She'd thought she was convenient. "There's a lot you don't know about me. You don't know my history."

Those gorgeous dark eyes of his rolled. "About your mom? Everyone knows that, Jules, and no one gives a shit. I don't watch her shows and I don't read her books. I don't care where you came from. I only care that you're here. And let's see what you know about me. You know I'm an asshole who fucks around. That means I couldn't possibly have feelings."

"Again, not what I said." And yet, somewhere deep down, hadn't that been what she'd thought? Hadn't she thought he was safe because he wasn't the kind of man who would want anything more than sex from her?

"Do you want to know the crazy thing? I still want you. Even knowing how you feel about me, I want you. After work, do you want to get together and fuck? Tonight's the night. I won't be able to for the rest of the week. I've got Rafe coming home and I need to stay at my place."

Her first instinct? Yes. Yes, she would like that very much. If he hadn't said all the other stuff, she would likely jump right into his bed. If she thought for a second they could keep this thing physical, she would, but he'd blown that out of the water. "Oh, Javi, that's not a good idea."

"So you had enough of me after one night?"

He needed to stop putting words in her mouth. "I can't tell you how much I needed that night."

His lips curled up faintly. "It was good."

"It was incredible. But we work together. It's not a good idea to get involved with people you work with."

"Ah, that's the argument. Kind of hard to use that here. Macon and Ally are married. Sebastian and Tiff are, too. Hell, Grace and Sean are married. We're just going to be fuck buddies so there's nothing to be worried about. I'm a big boy. Yeah, I was hurt, but now I know the score. You want sex. I want sex. We could have sex together. We live close and now we know to keep those pesky emotions out of the way. I'll be your coworker here and when we get home, if you've got an itch, I'll scratch it."

She hated how transactional the words sounded. "That sounds horrible."

"You got any better ideas because I can't get you out of my head. I wanted to date you, but I don't think that's in your plans."

None of this was in her plans. "I don't know what to do."

His face softened and he moved in close again. "Do what you want, Jules. Stop overthinking things and do what you want. You know where I am. If you want me, come and get me. I promise I won't even stay over. You won't have to kick me out in the morning."

For a second she thought he was going to kiss her. She started to go up on her toes because when he kissed her, she didn't think about anything but being with him. The world floated away and she needed that in the moment.

He stepped back. "I need to let the others back in or the ribs will dry out. Know that I would never affect your job. Whether or not you ever knock on my door again. I care about you. That doesn't change because you can't feel the same way about me. And be careful around the new cutting board. Those spikes are sharp as shit."

She glanced down and saw what he was talking about. It was a modified cutting board. She'd seen them on the Internet, but this was like the Cadillac of one-handed friendly tools. "Why do you have this?"

"I have a new chef coming in a few weeks. We're shuffling around a bit. He's got one hand, lost it during his service. I want to make things as easy on him as possible. Tried it myself. It's a pain in the ass, but I think with practice, he'll like it."

"You tried it?" She ran her fingers over the board. It was expertly crafted. It came in three parts; one seemed to detach. The better to scrape the cut veg into a container or the pan with one hand.

"I had Chef tie my hand down. It was rough. I'm shitty at it. I bet the new guy is phenomenal. Apparently he practices all the time. We're lucky to get him." He walked over to the door. "I'm sorry for the confusion, Jules. I'll explain to everyone that it was all my fault. Hell, they'll believe that."

"I didn't mean to hurt you."

He sighed, a tired sound that made her want to hug him. "We better get to work. And Jules, if you want to play around with that, feel free. I don't know how the new guy will feel about you using it after he gets here. You know how chefs can be possessive assholes about certain things. Especially the unique tools. They get it into their heads they're the only ones who can properly use something and they get pissy about anyone else touching it."

She turned to him. He was being nice and she'd been a complete bitch. What the hell was she supposed to do? "Javi, maybe we should…"

But the doors had come open and the crew was filing in.

"Thank god, the drama is over," Macon said. "You two work it all out? When's the wedding?"

Sometimes her coworkers were assholes.

"We're cool," Javier said "It was entirely a misunderstanding on my part. I apologized and we're moving on."

"Ah, so there's more drama coming." Macon shook his head and went back to making icing roses on his tiny cakes.

Javier went to his station and started pulling down a pan.

She wanted to talk to him, wanted to start the whole afternoon over. Maybe start the last few days over.

And do what? Fall into his arms? Pretend like they could really work?

She was ready to wade into the pool, not dive into the deep end.

And if that means the right one gets away? Because you were too scared? Because you decide when the time is right? It didn't work with Kevin so it wouldn't work with anyone?

As alive as she'd felt when she'd walked in, she felt dreary now. All those colors had gone back to gray and she wasn't sure what she should do.

She walked out of the kitchen and wished she'd never walked in. Naturally that was the moment Chef came out of his office and made a beeline in her direction.

"Here are the menus." Chef Taggart handed them over. "And if you could go over the reservations for the concert night dinner, I would appreciate it. We've got some bigwigs coming in. Apparently Wade Rycroft knows this singer, or at least she's a friend of a friend. He and Declan will be here for security. We need to plan on that, too."

Work. She needed to concentrate on work. "Of course."

Just when she thought Chef would dismiss her, let her go back to work, he frowned her way. "You really thought I would fire you? Because you slept with one of my line chefs? I've had a couple who were so wound up, I've offered to find hookers for them. There have been times I would have begged someone to sleep with those idiots. And if I fired everyone who slept with a coworker, I wouldn't have a staff. I swear the only place that's worse is my brother's office."

Another blush went through her. "I don't know what I thought. I couldn't think of another reason why you would call me into your office and I lost it."

"But you didn't lose it to me. It wasn't me you were shouting for. You went after Javier," Chef pointed out. "You went after him like a woman scorned, and I happen to know the man hasn't scorned you. It was enlightening. You got a strong streak of crazy bitch in there, O'Neil. It's good to know. I was worried about you for a while, but you let crazy bitch out enough and you'll be fine."

She was incredibly confused. "I disrupted your dinner prep. I still can't believe I did that."

"Yeah, you did. Think about that and why you did it and maybe you'll figure a few things out." He turned and went back into the kitchen.

The doors swung closed, but not before she caught a glimpse of Javi. He was starting a sauce of some kind, his face so serious. Everyone around him was joking, but he looked sad.

And that cutting board. She saw that, too.

She wasn't sure she would be able to stop thinking about either one of them.

Jules turned and found Tiffany and Ally watching her.

"You need to tell us that story. We can't stand it when the chefs know more than we do," Tiffany said.

It was going to be a long night.

Chapter Five

Javier pushed the wheelchair into his apartment, but not before he'd glanced at Jules's door. She hadn't shown up the night before. She hadn't even stayed for family supper. She'd been gone before he'd cleaned his station.

"The place doesn't look too bad," Rafe said as the door closed. "I thought you said someone trashed it."

Javier locked the door. "Someone did trash it. I have no idea why since they didn't take anything. I thought maybe some kids had gone around taking advantage of the storm to be little assholes, but from what I can tell I was the only apartment that got hit."

"You probably forgot to lock the door."

"I locked the door. I had a friend come out and look at the place. He thinks whoever broke in was looking for something." He didn't want to get into this with Rafe, but he had to. "Is there any reason someone would want to fuck with you?"

Rafe turned his head. "You're serious? This is my fault?"

Javier put his hands up, trying to stave off a heated conflict. "Not your fault. I was asking if anyone's threatened you. You're kind of an asshole now and you piss people off."

"Well, if they were pissed at me, shouldn't they have done something more than toss the furniture? It was probably kids looking for drugs. You see someone like me wheeling around like a pathetic chump and you know that's the dude who has the good drugs," Rafe reasoned.

The bathroom had been trashed. It was a logical conclusion. Besides, what else could he do about it? Brighton hadn't found anything. Nothing had been stolen. Because the security cameras had been out, there was no way to even track who'd come in and out of the complex. It seemed to be one of those crappy things that happened when you didn't live in a high-tech building.

He'd gotten permission to put in a better deadbolt. Jules would find she had permission as well.

"Speaking of, you get my meds?" Rafe's chair squeaked as he moved into the living room.

Javier had already stopped at the pharmacy. "I got them. I'll bring them to you in the morning. The doctor said he gave you everything you're supposed to take until morning."

Rafe's face tightened. "Doc doesn't know how much everything fucking hurts. I just went through surgery. You would think since I don't have any fucking legs I would hurt less."

"You went through surgery and you've had the pain medication the doctor prescribed. I'm not going to double dose you. The doc says if you would try to use what's left of your legs more, they would get strong and hurt less."

Rafe's head dropped back. "Stop telling me what the doctor says. I don't care what any of them say. They don't have to deal with those fucking prosthetics." His head came back up and he managed to wheel himself around to face Javier. "Did Sonja call?"

At least Rafe was asking about his wife. Ex-wife. It was still hard to think about her that way. He called her at least once a week to make sure she and his niece were all right. "I talked to her yesterday. She's doing all right. She got a new job."

Rafe's head came up, more interested in that information than he'd been in anything since Javier had picked him up. "Where is she working?"

It was the one bit of good news she'd had in a while. She'd seemed excited about it on the phone, a sparkle in her voice that had only died when she'd politely asked about Rafe. "She's at a law firm in Dallas. O'Malley and Taylor. It's a firm that specializes in corporate law. You know she finished her paralegal training after all these years."

He'd asked Sean if he knew any lawyers and soon Sonja had an interview. O'Malley and Taylor represented a large investment group Big Tag was a member of called the Masters Fund—run by the same man who was trying to poach Sean's chef—and Barnes and Fleetwood, a cattle rancher conglomerate. Sonja seemed to enjoy her new job and it paid well.

"Yeah, no thanks to me." Rafe sighed. "So she's working with a bunch of lawyers. You know if she's dating?"

Another subject he was careful to avoid. "Why do you care, man?"

"She's my wife."

"Ex-wife. You did that. You shoved her away." Javier moved to the kitchen. It was getting late and the nurse would be here soon. She was taking the night shift while Rafe recovered from surgery. "Do you want something to eat? I have to leave for work as soon as the nurse shows up and I won't be back until late."

"Not hungry." He was quiet for a moment. "I still love her. I never stopped loving her."

"Then why were you so awful to her?"

"Do you know what it's like to be someone one minute and in the next you're an entirely different human being, and you can't go back?" He pointed to the mantel over the fireplace where Javier kept pictures. There were framed shots of his mom and dad, some of he and Rafe as kids, a few of his niece, one of the original team at Top on the day the restaurant opened. But Rafe was pointing to the one of he and Sonja on their wedding day. Happy, shiny kids with their whole lives ahead of them. "I fucking hate that picture. I want you to burn it."

"I'll take it down if you want, but I'm not going to burn it. I love that picture. It reminds me of my brother."

A bitter laugh huffed from Rafe's mouth. "Yeah, the dead one because I'm not him, right?"

"Just shut up, Rafe. I don't want to have this conversation with you." He'd been avoiding it ever since Rafe had shown up on his doorstep.

"Because I'm not all content with life the way your one-armed girl is?" The question came out on a nasty huff. "You think I don't see how you look at her? She's always coming up to me when we're at PT and trying to be all sweetness and light. I see through her."

"Don't fucking talk about Jules."

Rafe smirked as though he knew he had him now. "I can talk about Jules all day, brother. I know her far better than you. I bet you buy her calm exterior. I bet you think she's really that content."

"I don't think she's content at all. I think she pretends and pretends, and I don't know how to make her stop and be real with me."

Rafe went still, his eyes focused for the first time in what felt like forever. "You like her."

He shouldn't have taken the bait. He should have kept his mouth shut. Rafe was toxic and tried to poison everything he touched. "I don't want to talk about it."

He started to move around his brother, but Rafe's hand shot out, holding his arm fast.

"I didn't realize you gave a shit about her. I'm sorry. She's a nice lady. I talk to her a lot, but you have to get that she's fucked up like me. She's not as cool as she seems to be. She's just way better at hiding it than I am."

"She doesn't push everyone away the way you do." Just him, and maybe he deserved it.

"I don't know about that. I think she would only push away the people who could hurt her. I'm sorry. I don't mean to make you feel like shit if she's close to you. Maybe she does like you. What do I know? I'm an idiot."

"You didn't used to be. You were the smartest guy I knew. You were the guy I went to when I needed advice. I need it now. I care about her. I...I'm really into Jules. Like I've never been into anyone before."

Rafe's eyes locked with his. "Don't. Let that one go because she's never going to want you. Not that she won't desire you, but she won't be with you. Never, man."

"Why? Because she sees me as some walking venereal disease?"

"No," Rafe replied. "Because she sees you as what she could have been. Like I said, I've talked to her a lot. She views you as everything she could have had, and she won't ever be able to forgive you for it."

Javi's knees felt weak because he realized what Rafe was saying. "Is that what happened with you and Sonja? You see her as what you could have been?"

He was quiet for a moment, but when he finally spoke, the words felt tortured. "I went into the military so I could go to school. You know that. Pops didn't have enough saved up for the education I needed. Sonja and I sat down and decided on how to get where we wanted to be. We decided on the military. I wanted to be a fucking lawyer. Isn't that rich? I should have taken the money Pops had and become a damn plumber. At least I'd have my legs. Who listens to a lawyer in a fucking wheelchair? How can I be anything when I can't walk? I can't get myself anywhere. I can't do anything for my damn self. But Sonja...oh, she can do it all."

He'd heard this argument from his brother a hundred times when he was drunk. "Because she's a badass bitch who doesn't let anything stand in her way. She does what needs to be done and she doesn't complain about it."

"Yeah? Well, she's never had to lose her legs."

Javier knew it was time to walk away, but he couldn't stop himself from arguing. "She lost her husband. She lost the love of her life and got back this whining, sad-sack baby who won't even try to live. Don't you dare say she's had it easy. She's raised a child without you. She lost you and you're still sitting here. And there are plenty of lawyers in wheelchairs. You lost your legs, not your brain. And don't think for a second I'm going to lose Jules the same way. I won't stop. She thinks I'm something she can't be. I'll prove to her otherwise."

"You'll lose. She's lost. She can smile and shit, but she's exactly like the rest of us," Rafe spat out. "She should have died. It would have been a kindness."

"Fuck you. Start thinking about where else you can go because I'm not going to let you stay here if you can say that." Javi'd had enough. He turned and walked back out the front door and into the hallway. He couldn't look at whatever devil now inhabited Rafe's skin. That thing lived to sow chaos, to see the people around him miserable.

He put his back to the wall and let himself sink to the floor. What the fuck was he going to do?

He couldn't put his brother out on the street.

He let his head drift to his hand, misery welling inside him. He'd loved his brother. How did he deal with who his brother had become?

Was Rafe right about Juliana? Was there some festering sore deep inside her that couldn't be fixed? Was he setting himself up for heartache?

"Javi?"

He looked up and she was standing there, a watery vision in the hallway.

She dropped the grocery bag she was holding and sank down beside him, her arm going around his shoulders. "Rafe's back, then?"

He couldn't even answer her, merely let himself sag against her.

"I'm sorry, Javi. He doesn't mean half of what he says. He feels bad so he's mean to the people he cares about, the ones he knows won't go away, and even some of them leave him," she whispered. "I'm sorry."

He wasn't sure what she was apologizing for, but he welcomed her warmth. She wasn't lost. Even in her pain and fumbling, she was kind. She wanted to be loved. She simply wasn't sure how to ask for it, and he was a fool who didn't know what he was doing either. Jules deserved better than him.

They sat there for a while, her arm around him, their heads touching.

"Should I give up on you?" Javier asked.

She was silent and he thought she would stand up and walk away, but then her hand slid over his, tangling their fingers together. "I would rather you didn't."

She went silent again and he was content to sit with her hand in his.

* * * *

"You need to rethink this. Come on, give it a shot. It's fun." Deena grinned as she put the finishing touches on her makeup for the evening. "We've been having this party once a month ever since we bought the house. I know we could go to Sanctum and we do, but sometimes it's fun to not have to make the drive. We keep everything pretty casual."

"This does not feel casual." Jules squirmed as Kori pulled on the laces of the emerald green corset they'd selected for this venture. It looked gorgeous on the mannequin, but then the mannequin didn't have nerves and skin, and no one had tied her in like a sausage roll. Her only other clothing? A tiny little matching thong. "And you did get the part where I'm probably not going to stay very long."

"Don't be such a baby," Kori said as she tightened the laces again. "You look gorgeous."

"But I'm going to tell the guy Kai assigned me to that I changed my mind," she complained. "Shouldn't I do that in street clothes? Won't this give him the wrong idea?"

Ally looked up from the vanity she was sitting at. Apparently on play party nights, Deena turned the Master bedroom into the women's locker room. "Why are you copping out on him again?"

"Because she's scared," Deena shot back.

"I am not." She was, but not as scared as she'd been before. "It doesn't feel right."

"I think it's because she loves therapy," Kori explained. "She can't stand the thought of missing out on a session with my man. He'll do that to you. You get addicted to the way he adjusts his glasses."

She had to smile. "That's it. I can't go a week without opening my heart and soul to Kai."

Tiffany looked perfect in her leather catsuit, her long legs well defined. "I think she doesn't want to hurt Javi's feelings. Or she doesn't want to watch Javier scene with another chick."

The idea kind of turned her stomach. "I'm very confused when it comes to Javier, and that means I should take a step back."

Don't rush into something, baby girl. Give it time and think about what you want and what's the best way to achieve your goal. Talk to me. I'll help you make a plan.

Yeah, she couldn't talk to her mom anymore, but slowing down still seemed like a good thing to do. When she'd found Javier sitting in the hallway, she hadn't even hesitated. There had been no question in her head that she would walk by. She'd done what felt right. She'd gotten down on the floor with him and offered him comfort.

And when he'd asked about giving up on her, she hadn't been able to take the out.

"What's confusing about Javi?" Deena asked. "He's totally upfront."

Ally frowned her friend's way. "I don't know about that. He's being kind of sneaky with her. I think it means he likes her. Like *like* likes her."

Tiffany shook her head. "Don't listen to Ally. She eats way too much sugar. What she's trying to say is that Javier has never been serious about a woman before and might never be again. He's an honest guy. If he tells you something, you can believe him."

Like saying she was special. "And if I'm not ready?"

The last woman in the room stood up and smoothed down her long dark hair. Sarah Stevens looked at herself in the mirror. "Then you should be prepared to make yourself ready or lose the right one forever because the right one doesn't always sit at home pining for you and hoping you'll change your mind. She doesn't sit around watching your television show and eating ice cream and dreaming about your abs. She goes and finds newer, more attentive abs, abs that are prepared to accept the affection you have to give them."

Sarah walked out, her heels clicking on the floor.

"Javier doesn't have a TV show," Jules said, looking to Kori for more information.

"See, Sarah started out with the right idea and then veered totally off into personal territory," Kori said with a sigh. "Don't mind her. She's dealing with the fact that her right guy wasn't ready when she was."

"I heard a rumor that she had a thing for an actor," Ally said.

"Kai's brother. He used to be on TV. He's been floating around since the end of the show. I hoped he would come home, but he's having trouble trusting people," Kori said. "And I think he'll lose her over it. I think it's there in the back of his mind that she'll be waiting for him when he's ready, but Sarah is not one to sit around and hope a guy comes to his senses. She's moved on. She started dating a doctor she met at work. He's an asshat. I hate him and I'm pretty sure one of these days he's going to ask her to marry him and she's going to say yes."

"People can't help bad timing." Wasn't that what was going on with Javier? Bad timing. She wasn't ready. He was.

Would she be ready if he had any other job? If he wasn't so damn good at the one he had? If he was an accountant, would she have jumped in with both feet?

Was she torturing herself by working at Top? By staying close to what she wanted? How was she going to feel when the one-handed chef came in? What the hell was that about? What kind of experience did that guy have? Had he grown up in kitchens?

She forced the thought back as she had been for doing for days.

"The timing is always bad," Tiffany said. "That's life. There's always some reason to say no. The key is not being able to. It's about finding that one man who you can't say no to because he's wormed his way into your heart. Sebastian didn't think it was the right time either. I convinced him. And Kori got over her fear of the man bun and now she and Kai are very happy."

"His man bun is sexy," Kori advised. "If I don't say that he won't whip me tonight, and this girl needs some serious relaxation." She finished up and turned Jules toward the mirror. "There you go. Now you look amazing and you'll properly honor the dude you're turning down for the night."

Yeah. She would honor him with her boobs. Her boobs looked awesome. The emerald made her skin glow. It was perfectly creamy and smooth right to the point where her prosthetic was attached.

Deena stepped in front of her, reaching for her hand, the fake one. She held it like it still had feeling. "If he can't see how gorgeous you are, he doesn't deserve you."

Ally moved in beside her. "It took forever to convince Macon he should wear shorts and show off how intensely hot his body is, but I managed it. You're beautiful, Jules."

"No one out there will think anything less," Tiffany promised. "And if they do, we'll weed 'em out. This whole party is about having fun and accepting who we are. There's no one way to be beautiful. So show them your way."

Her way. She looked at herself again. She was good at pretending to be cool with her life. But what was really unattractive about her arm? It wasn't normal, but it worked. Not as well as it had, but she could be independent.

Adaptation. That word kept playing through her head.

"Is Javier here tonight?" She'd intended to speak to the Dom Kai had selected to be her guide and then head home. She needed time to think about what she wanted. To carefully lay out all the options. The last time she'd done something without planning, she'd ended up in the Navy, and where had that gotten her?

It had gotten her to a place where she could save five lives. Would she let those lives go to save her hand?

Was there ever a right time for anything? A right time? A right place? A right man?

"I saw his truck pull up," Tiffany replied.

Deena winced. "I hope he's ready because Kristy came tonight, too, and I think she's decided he's still her best bet. Sorry, guys. She's close friends with Eric's sous chef's sub, and we're desperately trying to keep him."

"Damn," Ally swore. "I'll go and run interference."

"Interference?" Jules asked.

Tiffany stood to go with Ally. "Kristy can be very aggressive and Javier...well, when he's not attached...I don't think I've ever seen him attached. He tends to take whatever's offered, if you know what I mean."

She shook her head. "Not with that one. She walked out on him when he needed her. He won't be going back to her. Not even for sex."

Deena looked a bit uncertain. "I'm glad you believe in him."

The guys liked to bet. Maybe it was time she did show some faith in him. "Twenty bucks says he turns her down flat."

Deena's eyes narrowed. "I don't know if taking that bet makes me a bad person, but I'm in. Especially if it means you stay for a bit."

There was the trap and she'd walked right into it. But then maybe she'd wanted to. Kai wanted her to do one thing that scared her. Well, nothing scared her quite like Javier.

"Don't bother running interference. Javier can handle that woman," she said. "And someone help me get my arm off. I don't need it tonight."

She didn't like the way the suspension system looked. It wasn't that it was ugly, merely that she thought her skin was prettier.

"You don't have to do that," Kori said. "I'm telling you no one minds here."

Jules was sure Kristy minded, but she would mind the stump, too. It wasn't about that. "I don't need it tonight. I'm going to ask Javier to show me around and he'll take care of me. It will be nice to depend on someone else for a night."

Kori's lips curled up. "That is an excellent reason to dump the arm. And you are playing Xbox this week."

Ten minutes later she walked out into the large living area and couldn't help but gawk like the tourist she was. "It's really pretty."

Deena stayed close to her side. "Not what you expected, huh?"

"It's not very dungeon like." The room had been done in multicolored twinkle lights. All the furniture had been rearranged and covered in what looked like incredibly soft blankets. There were already couples relaxing and talking quietly.

"The dining room is much more of a scene space," she agreed. "And then there's our actual playroom, where most of the scenes will happen. I've got a violet wand set up in one of the guest bedrooms, and there are a couple of spanking benches. The kitchen has a nice buffet and wine and beer, but be careful. If Eric thinks someone's playing drunk, he'll take care of that pretty damn quick."

Kai stepped out of the kitchen and smiled her way. "You look lovely tonight, Jules. I'm happy to see you here. I think I saw Cal in the dining room. Let me introduce the two of you."

"Cal is not needed this evening," a familiar voice said.

She turned and her mouth nearly dropped open. Javier was standing there dressed in a pair of jeans that molded to his every muscle and nothing else. His chest was on full display and it was stunning. She'd seen it before, but she hadn't had the real chance to simply stare at him.

"Someone has to walk her around," Kai said, eyeing Javi, though she was fairly certain it wasn't with the same amount of lust she had. "Are you planning on handling those duties tonight?"

"I will." He turned toward her. His hand came out, seeking to shake hers. She put out her good hand, but Javier was too quick. He reached straight for her left arm and brought her stump to his lips.

That man knew how to get to her. "So you got rid of my mentor for the night?"

"I am giving you an alternative," he promised. "And I swear, I'll keep my hands to myself. I'll be a good mentor and I'll even drive you home. I'll answer your every question and behave myself."

She could barely breathe. How had she thought she could stay away from him? Why would she want to stay away from him?

Oh, yeah, there was the whole danger to her heart and well-being, but somehow she couldn't think about that in the moment. All she could see was his chest and abs. Sarah had talked about finding a nice set of abs to settle down with for the night and that suddenly seemed like a brilliant idea.

"Jules?" Kai was staring at her expectantly. "Do you accept Javier as your mentor for the night? He's gone through all the training classes. He knows what he's doing and I trust him. I could go over some of the classes he's trained in."

Kori put a hand on her husband's chest. "Stop teasing her. The drool is totally a sign of acceptance."

Was she really drooling?

"I can't help it," Kai said with a grin that made him look far younger. "Come on, love. Eric's got a hard point in the garage for suspension play."

There was no way to miss the light in Kori's eyes as she let her husband lead her away.

"You two have fun," Deena said. "I'm going to help Eric in the kitchen and then we're going to play. See you around."

"Are you sure it's all right?" Javier stepped in so she could hear him over the music. It wasn't loud, but neither was Javier.

She stared up at him. That was one gorgeous man. "You planned this."

"Yeah. I told Cal I would murder him if he laid hands on you."

"You were sneaky." Everything the women had said to her came back full force. Javier was upfront. He didn't expend energy he didn't have to. If he wanted a casual hookup, he would find one.

She was difficult. And he was still here.

"I have to be when it comes to you," he admitted. "But I think you're going to be worth it. You already are. Did I thank you for sitting with me the day Rafe came home? I swear I never realized how lonely I was until I met you."

He was going to kill her. "I don't know that this is the best idea, Javi, but I know I want to try. I can't seem to not try. Why don't we take it slow?"

He backed up slightly. "Slow. I can do that."

"But we could play around with this stuff, right? I mean they call it play for a reason. It's not super serious."

"That's not necessarily true." He took her hand and led her toward the kitchen. "Come with me. We need to talk before we start the evening."

She should have known that anything that was Kai-approved would come with a whole lot of talking. She followed Javier as he walked through the double doors that led to the kitchen. It looked like this was a part of the house Eric had either renovated or it was the reason he'd bought the sucker. The kitchen was huge, with a massive island and professional-grade appliances.

She stared at that gleaming six-burner gas stove and then realized it was Javi's turn to drool. They were dressed for sex, but she and Javier were lusting after an appliance.

"One of these days," he said with a sigh.

"One of these days," she replied.

"Now we're talking, baby. Come here."

Why had she said that? She didn't need a six-burner stove. And yet for a second she saw herself standing there, flipping something in a ridiculously perfect pan. She'd been standing next to Javier and they'd worked flawlessly together.

That way lay danger. She was about to say something, draw her hand away from his, but she caught sight of Ian Taggart sitting in the corner. He was dressed in leathers, but his attention was focused on the woman sitting in his lap. His wife was in a corset and thong, but he wasn't looking at her breasts. Nope. His whole attention was focused on what was in her hand.

"Is that one of Macon's lemon tarts?" Jules asked quietly.

Javier leaned over to whisper. "Yeah, he made them special for tonight. It keeps Big Tag happy. Last week he sent over a gallon of lemon pudding. I do not want to know what those two did with that. I highly suspect it was nasty."

Charlotte Taggart took a bite of the tart and then licked her lips.

"Only you, baby," Big Tag whispered back. It was super sensual, the way they shared the decadent treat. Charlotte held the tart up to her husband's lips, but at the last second, he pulled her in instead and took her mouth in a ridiculously dominant move.

Just watching them was getting her hot. And she didn't think Big Tag was all that sexy. Sure he was gorgeous, but he was never serious. He was really serious about kissing his wife.

Javier led her to the backdoor. He tugged her along until she found herself in the backyard. It was small but lovely, with an outdoor kitchen and a ten-foot privacy fence. The light from the small pool illuminated the yard with a blue glow.

"That's better. If we stayed in the kitchen, I'm fairly certain you would have seen your first hard-core sex scene," he admitted. "Those two are known for being terrible exhibitionists."

"They're going to have sex right there in the kitchen?" She glanced back, oddly wondering if she shouldn't have watched that.

He sat down on the plush lounge chair. "Yes. They will and they won't have any shame about it. This is a space where they don't have to. No one here will think any less of them. It works for them as a couple. They can be lovers in a space like this, not limited to their bedroom. They've got three kids. Apparently, that's hell on a sex life, but they can come here and be crazy lovers for a while. And that's something I think we should talk about."

"Being crazy lovers?"

"The fact that we've got several relationships going on, and I didn't think about it when I came to you the first night. I'll be honest—I didn't think I would get any further than sitting with you and sharing a bottle of wine and asking you if you wanted to go out with me sometime."

She let him tug her down beside him and felt a smile cross her face. It was good to know she could be surprising. "Shocked you, huh?"

"I was very happy, but now I realize I gave myself away far too quickly. You view me as a sexual object."

He sounded so prim, she had to bite back a laugh. "I'm very sorry, Javier. I used you for sex and that was wrong of me."

He brought her hand to his mouth and kissed her palm. "You know how ridiculous that sounds, but I didn't like the way you dismissed me the next day. I know I have a reputation, but I have feelings for you. I want a promise that if we decide to sleep together again, you'll stay in bed with me, wake up with me, spend the morning with me."

"I promise." She didn't like the thought that he had felt used. Even though that's kind of what she'd done. "But like I said, I'm not sure I'm ready for anything serious."

Because she was scared and she had to wonder if her fear was going to cost her everything.

"I think we need boundaries," Javier said. "I'm your boss at work. Not directly, of course, but Chef is giving me more responsibilities, and I might need your help from time to time."

She wouldn't mind taking more responsibility for the front of house. No matter what Kai said, she was adapting. She couldn't cook the way she wanted so she would concentrate on other parts of the industry she loved. "I can handle that."

"Excellent," he continued. "We're friends when we leave work and we can decide what we want to be when we're here."

"At Deena's house?"

"When we're playing," he corrected. "When we're at a party like this or when I bring you to Sanctum."

"I thought you were holding off taking someone to the big club."

"I was holding off with Kristy. I'll take you in a heartbeat. I trust you." Javier leaned back, relaxing. "So, I want you to think about what you want from me here. It's okay if all you want is a mentor, but if you're interested in the lifestyle, let me train you. I'm going to admit that I'm not a full-time top. I enjoy it sexually, but in real life I don't want anything that's close to twenty-four seven."

"I don't think I would need that kind of top. By the way, who says I'm not a top?"

A sexy grin crossed his face. "Says the man who recently made love to you. My darling, that sex might have been fairly vanilla, but you responded perfectly every time I took control. I want you to think about a specific scenario, and this is one that would take place in the D/s part of our relationship."

"A scenario?" Jules asked.

"Yes, this is the play part of playing. I enjoy role-play. I want you to imagine that you're a secretary. My secretary. Unfortunately, you've made a terrible mistake that costs the company money. You enter my office, desperate to save your job."

She wrinkled her nose. "This doesn't sound particularly sexy."

"Oh, but that's because you don't know where I'm going with it. You see, I've been watching you, Miss O'Neil. The way I look at it, I've got two choices. I could call the police in and have them take you away or I can decide if it was all merely a mistake. I think the only way I would be able to trust you again is to bind you to me. How do you think I'm going to bind you to me? To tie you so closely to me that I don't have to worry about you betraying me again?"

Sex. Naturally he would use sex. She could see herself. She would be dressed in a prim business suit, tears in her eyes when he suggested another way out of their problem. "What would you do?"

She wanted to hear him say the words.

"I would sit back in my chair and explain to you that your duties have changed and that means you'll need a new uniform. Tell me something, Miss O'Neil, are you wearing underwear? Because I don't think your new duties require those."

"You're a pervert, Leones," she said, but she was feeling the heat.

"Am I? Tell me something else," he said, his voice low and deep. He leaned in, his mouth close to her ear. "If I ran my hand up your thigh and let my fingers find your pussy, would it be wet? Did thinking about me having sexual control over you get you hot or did you find it distasteful? Does the thought of being in my power, of serving me in that fashion, knowing that I would be a kind Master and ensure your safety and pleasure, does that do something for you? Because I can smell you right now and I'll know if you're lying to me. Lying to your mentor could bring about unexpected consequences. Now, who do you think you are in this part of our relationship?"

All the air seemed to have fled her lungs. He was so close their mouths were almost together. "I'm the sub. Definitely the sub."

"Yes, you are."

She closed her eyes, ready to let him lead her in this. Boundaries. They would have boundaries, and that made her feel safe.

"All right, let's go watch some scenes and then we can talk."

She opened her eyes and he was standing over her, his hand out to help her up. What had happened? He wanted to watch other people and talk some more?

He smiled like he could tell exactly what she was thinking. "It's part of the process, sweetheart. Let me lead you in this section. We'll talk about how you want to proceed. Remember this. You're the sub and that means ultimately you're in control."

It was weird and intriguing.

And she found herself walking back into the kitchen next to him.

Javier stopped her, stepping in front of her body. "What the hell happened?"

Big Tag and Charlotte were on the floor, a tangle of body parts and lemon desserts.

"Don't you take the arrow out," Charlotte was yelling into her cell phone even as she tried to stay completely still.

"You tell him I will kill him if this incident scars my baby girl for life," Ian swore. "Charlie, baby, my shoulder's out of socket. Could you help me out?"

Without missing a beat, she scrambled to her feet, leaned down, selected one of the unspoiled tarts and shoved it into her husband's mouth. "Happy now? I told you that chair wouldn't hold us both and it's the babysitter who got shot. Boomer might die on our living room floor." She was back on the phone. "I'm sorry. We're on our way right now. Seriously, don't take that arrow out."

Big Tag was on his feet, chewing the last of the tarts even as his arm was at a completely unnatural angle. "Macon! Buddy, I'm going to need these to go. Date night's fucked up again. Javi, some help here?"

Javier shook his head and put out an arm, bracing himself. "Has anyone ever told you you're completely insane?"

Big Tag grinned and used Javier's straight arm to shove his shoulder back into socket with an audible crack. "Never heard that one before. Use condoms. Like three of 'em."

He turned and followed his wife out.

"First scene of the night," Javier said with a shake of his head. "Let's see if we can find one that's less crazy. Let's go watch the sadist. It's probably less violent than what we just saw."

She held his hand and let him lead her away.

Chapter Six

She was here and that was all he could ask.

Javier watched as the scene started to wind down. Kai and Kori could go at it pretty hard, which was precisely why he'd brought her out to the garage to watch their scene. Kori didn't hold back. She howled and cursed her Master and giggled and laughed, and when she came he was surprised the neighborhood couldn't hear it.

He was throwing her in the deep end, but she needed to see what it was like.

"I don't think I'll ever look at my therapist the same way again," she admitted as they stepped back into the house. She stopped, seeing that Eric had Deena tied to a St. Andrew's Cross and was using a flogger on her.

It was a lot. Maybe he should have gone slower.

"Any questions?" Or would you prefer to run screaming from the house?

She turned and grinned up at him, a light in her eyes. "What can I try?"

He breathed an audible sigh of relief. "I thought I scared you off."

"It looks fun. I don't think I'm ready for suspension play, but I get some of it," she replied. "It's about stimulating parts of your body that don't get stimulated often. I realized that there's this part of PT I always look forward to. I thought it was weird and maybe a little perverse at first, but I always want to tell the guy who puts the TENS on my arm to turn that sucker up. It's feeling where there was none before. I like it."

Oh, he knew what they should play with. "Come on. Let's see if anyone's using the violet wand. I don't know if they have a TENS here, but this should work."

He'd turned away earlier. When she'd closed her eyes, he'd known he could have kissed her. Hell, he likely could have laid her back on the chaise and had his way with her, but they would have been right back at the start. She knew he could handle her sexually. He had to prove he could be more than a walking, talking vibrator.

He ducked into the guest bedroom where he knew Eric had set up the violet wand. He was in luck. It was quiet in here and it looked like everyone had been busy with suspension and impact play. He picked up the wand and attached a head, this one a flat glass piece.

"Normally, we would sit down and negotiate a contract between the two of us and I would go over what kinds of play you're interested in and what your hard and soft limits are."

"But I don't know anything, so I have no idea."

"Trust me, you could answer some of them very quickly," he said with a chuckle. "And if you want to pursue this past tonight, we'll need something in place between us. But for now we're just going to play around, and if at any time you're scared, tell me and I'll stop."

Her pretty blue eyes rolled in a perfectly bratty expression of disdain. "You're not going to scare me with that wand thingee. I was in the Navy, you know. Not exactly a fainting flower."

It was one of the things that made him want her. "Okay, then. This is what we call a violet wand. It sends an electrical charge across your skin."

"Fun," she said.

"And stimulating." That was the point. He flicked the wand on and the air suddenly smelled like ozone as the glass held a purple charge. He set it on the lowest setting and tested it. Like everything Eric owned, it was well taken care of and did its job. "Let me see your arm."

She started to hold out her whole arm.

"Nope. The other one." It was the one she tried not to use, the one that got the least stimulation.

She bit her bottom lip but did as he asked.

He let the sound crackle through the air. "So this is a low setting. It should feel like bubbles over your skin. I'm not going to play it over the surgical adhesions. It's a little different than a TENS and I want to avoid anywhere with nerve damage. That's fun you'll have to have in PT."

He ran the wand over her skin, starting at her elbow and skimming it down to just above where the limb ended. He was rewarded with a shiver and a smile.

"It does feel like bubbles," she said. "You know you're the only person outside of my doctors who ever touch me there. You can take it higher. I think I'd like more."

He upped the wattage slightly. He held her arm with one hand as he played the wand over her. "This should feel like a caress of light. I think more people would if you let them in. It's not that anyone cares. They simply don't feel close enough to touch you."

"I think your friend Kristy would disagree," she replied with a gasp. She grinned, obviously enjoying the sensation.

"Turn around." He could light her up if that was what she liked. He pulled her hair to one side, loving the silky feel of it against his palm. "Kristy is a person who doesn't matter. If you need the world to be with you, Jules, you're going to be disappointed. I've learned to make my world small and filled with people who count. Even then they can disappoint you because at the end of the day we're all human and make terrible mistakes."

Her head turned, eyes coming up to meet his. "I was putting her name out there because I heard she was here and I was jealous."

Sweet honesty. They were making progress. "She came on to me.

I sent her away in no uncertain terms. I know who she is. There might have been a time when I would have taken what she offered, but it's gone now."

She turned her head to face front, but not before he'd seen the satisfied smirk on her lips. Confident and sexy. "Deena owes me twenty bucks."

He should protest, but apparently she'd bet on him. He brushed his fingers over the nape of her neck. "I'm glad I came through for you. How do you like this?"

He cranked it up slightly and ran it over her nape and down her spine.

Her head fell forward. "I like it, Javi. I like it a lot. It feels good."

The husky sound of her voice went straight to his cock. The new plan sucked. The new plan required him to be patient, to not throw her down on the first convenient horizontal surface and fuck her like she was the last woman on earth. Nope. He wasn't going to do that because he'd done that before and it hadn't brought about the result he wanted.

"I'm glad. I like playing with the wand, too." He ran it down both her arms, enjoying the way she responded. He got down on one knee. Damn, she had the prettiest ass. He couldn't possibly let her know how easy it had been to tell Kristy he wasn't interested. She'd shown up in her most angelic white corset, her blonde hair a halo around her face. She'd been beautiful but in a calculating way. She'd had nothing on his Jules, with her wavy red hair and guileless eyes. And this ass. He brought the wand just below the curve of her ass and she jumped.

"Hold still or I could hurt you," he warned. "Hold on to the table."

There was a good-sized massage table in the room, and he had to wonder if Eric was thinking of opening his own damn club. The man definitely had a hobby. She leaned over and put her hand on the table, stabilizing herself.

He ran the wand all over her legs, making lines of light down to her feet. She squirmed and wiggled, and every gasp made his cock tighten because he knew it was all prepping her. Prepping her for something he couldn't give her.

He was going to masturbate like crazy tonight. He was going to grip his own dick and stroke himself, thinking about her the entire time. He would go over every filthy way he could have her and do it again and again until he could think straight around her.

"The violet wand can be especially fun. Did you know if you held a light bulb in your hand and I got close enough with the wand, you could light it up?" Javier asked, trying to keep his mind on the task at hand. He was mentoring her, teaching her about how fun play could be. Maybe a few weeks from now they could move this section of their relationship to the next level.

Boss/employee, neighbors, mentor/trainee. He had to take it slow so he could move them along to coworkers, true friends, lovers. Goals. A man had to have goals and had to be patient enough to reach them.

"That would be fun," she said, her voice shaky. "I can see where this would be a fun scene to watch or play around in. But Javier, I would like to feel this all over. It's nice on my arms and legs. What would it be like in other places?"

Fuck him. It would be incredibly hot. It would be sexy as hell. His dick would explode in his jeans and he would look like the biggest idiot on the planet. Doms were supposed to be in control even when they were only Doms in a play space. And yet, it was his job to serve her this evening, to let her explore the boundaries. She'd been incredibly open and tolerant up to this point. He couldn't not reward her sweet curiosity—even if it meant leaving himself in a very bad place. But then who hadn't walked around a dungeon with a massive, not-going-to-get-any-relief-tonight hard-on?

Still, she might not understand that he couldn't touch her over her clothes. "I can't get too close to the corset, sweetheart. It's got metal in it and that would conduct the electricity in a way that wouldn't be fun."

"That's okay. I would love to take it off."

Yes. He was going to die. "Jules, I can get you out of that corset, but I'm not good at putting clothes back on a woman. It was never my goal. If I take you out of it, you'll have to walk around half naked the rest of the night."

She was quiet for a moment, the hum of the wand the only sound between them. "I saw lots of boobs and dicks and butts today. I was surprised that it didn't bother me. It felt okay, like I was just getting to know people better."

"Because they're comfortable with it and they don't make a big deal out of it," he replied. It was going to be pure hell to get her naked and not touch her with anything except the wand, but then he'd made his bed by jumping into hers without setting the ground rules. "So do you want to play more?"

"Unless it would bother you." Self-consciousness was creeping into her tone and he hated that. She'd found a confidence while they'd walked around that had been a lovely thing to see.

"It won't bother me at all." It would make him crazy. He would spend the rest of the evening attempting to leash his inner caveman. He flicked off the violet wand and put it down on the table. "Let's get you out of this."

He loosened the laces, easing them out. She looked gorgeous in the corset, but her skin was lovelier, and that night they'd spent together had been too quick. He'd been so eager he'd only taken a few moments to look at her before he'd gotten his mouth on her. This time, with no expectation of sex, he could take his time and appreciate her beauty.

Maybe it wouldn't be bad. Anticipation. He needed to get used to it. He managed to loosen the laces enough that he could ease the corset over her. Her hair spilled down her back, making her look like some mermaid he'd caught, one who he'd never throw back, so he needed to figure out how to take care of this mysterious, gorgeous creature because she was his.

He couldn't stop himself from reaching out to brush his fingers over the grooves the tight corset had left in her skin. Those were lovely, too.

She relaxed under his hands. "That feels even better than the wand."

He chuckled but ran his palms over her back. "That's because you probably are taking your first full breath in a couple of hours. Fet wear can be part of the torture. The crazy thing is once you've stopped torturing yourself, the act of getting undressed feels satisfying and pleasurable."

"And free."

"And free." He gathered all that hair and brushed it to one side. "How free do you want to be? How far do you want me to go? There's no metal in your thong. You can keep that on if you like."

"I don't. Like, that is. I think I want to be naked. I like how I feel when I'm naked and you look at me."

Those words threatened to split him open, and he decided then and there to give her everything she wanted and to take nothing for himself. She needed to understand how much he was willing to give her, how far he wanted them to go.

"Then I would like for you to take them off and give them to me. I'll keep them until you need them again. If you feel like you need them again." He needed to get her used to the whole Dom/sub byplay thing. Her clothes would be something they would play with. He would demand them or leave them on as he would. He would build the anticipation or strip her bare so she could feel the cool air on her skin right before he slapped her ass and got her hot.

She hesitated, but only for a few seconds, and then she turned around, showing him her breasts. Her eyes met his and she slowly hooked her thumb under the waistband of her thong and tugged it down those long, luscious legs of hers. She straightened up and held them out. "Here you go, Sir."

Fuck. He'd played around at this, enjoyed the fun of helping lovely women find their sexualities, but the way she called him *Sir* twisted something deep inside him. In a really good, warm, this-is-what-I-waited-for way. He took her undies and slid them in his pocket.

"Again, before tonight I would have found that incredibly weird, but now that I know Tiffany lets Sebastian use a butt plug on her, you carrying my thong around in your pocket feels perfectly normal."

And that was the whole point. It felt good to bring her into this world, and she would find the women would be even more open with her now that she'd been here and accepted them. "What you don't know is last week Tiff mouthed off one too many times about Sebastian's choice of Riesling and she spent all Thursday dinner service with a butt plug. Never lost it once, even when every Dom in the place made it hard on her. That was Sebastian's request, by the way. He wanted a pile on."

"I wondered why they kept dropping things and not being able to get it themselves. They managed to always be cooking when something slipped away. Bastards." But she giggled.

He patted the massage table. It was covered with a super-soft blanket. "Hop up here. Flat on your back."

She immediately did as he'd ordered, her eagerness soothing to his soul. They could at least have this. If he was the one to introduce her to the lifestyle, she might bond to him in a way that would keep her by his side.

He had to stare for a moment. Goddess in repose. So fucking beautiful. He brought the wand up. "I'm sticking to the mushroom electrode. It's best in the beginning, but if you like, next time we'll use one with a smaller head. The feeling will be much more focused and intense the smaller the head."

He clicked it on and her whole body jumped slightly. Ah, the mindfuck. She was responding beautifully to the mindfuck and that meant one thing. She trusted him. Jules wasn't an adrenaline junkie. She didn't do things for the scare. She enjoyed this because she trusted him not to hurt her.

Life had been easier when he hadn't cared. And it had been much, much emptier. "I want to show you something. Close your eyes."

"How can you show me if I can't see?"

Such a brat. "I could spank you. I'll find a mirror and you can see that."

Her eyes closed. "You're a very serious mentor."

He never had been before, but he would give it to her. He was damn serious about her. He turned up the wattage because he could take a lot more than she could and touched it to his chest. The light sparked through him, stimulating him. He leaned over and brushed his lips against hers.

She shivered when the spark went from him to her, her eyes flying open.

He stood back up, a smile on his face. Yeah, his dick was dying, but he loved playing with her. "See, sparks fly when we kiss. Now hold on. If you move too much, I'll have to tie you down."

Not that he would mind. She would look lovely in bondage. Though he would have to figure out how to properly and safely bind her left arm. He would ask Chef about it. Sean knew more about rope than he did.

It seemed like somehow his whole life had become about ensuring her safety, plotting how to bring her closer, planning a future he'd never thought he would have.

If only he could make her see what he did.

It all began with bringing her pleasure. He brought the wand down and put his plan into action.

* * * *

Jules held on to the blanket beneath her and felt her toes curl as Javier brought the wand down to her breast. There was a crackling sound as it hit her skin and then the hum of electricity as he made patterns. She could see the purple spark that flashed against her and lit up her flesh.

Who would have thought electrical play would be her thing? Then again, who the hell would have guessed that Juliana O'Neil would be into kinky sex? Because it turned out she was really into kinky sex.

There had been a time when she'd been sure she wasn't into any kind of sex at all. It hadn't bothered her when she and Kevin were away from each other. After the accident and divorce, she'd thought she could live without it entirely until that moment she'd seen Javier.

This was their place to be sensual. Every move he made with that damn wand forced her body to clench and release and relax. She couldn't remember a time when she'd felt so free. No one at the party had looked at her like she was a freak. Here she wasn't her mother's daughter, and she wasn't the sum of her lost body parts. She was just Jules.

She could be Master Javier's submissive. That suddenly seemed like a good thing to be.

They would have rules and boundaries and he would be honest with her. She wouldn't have to worry about how he felt because when he was acting as her Dominant partner, it was his responsibility to tell her the truth.

Hadn't he been that way the whole time?

She couldn't stop the gasp that came out of her mouth when he touched the wand to her nipple. It was like her whole body lit up at the touch, as though he'd found a conduit that could send flash fire through her. Somehow the momentary flare of shock turned into warmth, curling through her and making her every muscle limp.

He moved to the other nipple, playing with her body and making it very hard for her to stay still. That, it seemed, was part of the torture for her.

Javier made a long, slow exploration of her body, running the wand over her in patterns that kept her guessing. Every touch felt new, every one different.

She didn't want this to end.

She had to remember where they were and that they couldn't make the same mistake again. What were the words he would use? "Javier, can we negotiate?"

She watched his face tighten.

"I don't know if that's a good idea." He shut off the wand and laid it back in its case. "Let me take care of you and then we can go somewhere to talk."

She sat up, looking at the huge tent in his jeans. "Shouldn't I take care of you, too?"

"Again, not a good idea." He moved toward her, his face

softening. "But I will take care of you. Let me touch you."

She held out her hand. "But you don't want me to touch you."

Maybe she shouldn't feel so comfortable naked.

"It doesn't mean the same thing to you that it means to me," he explained in a quiet voice.

"So you won't make love to me unless I'm in love with you? I thought that was why we had the boundaries. So we could figure out if we work. So we would have a place that was safe to be together in."

He stopped, the playful persona he often wore failing him. "I don't like it when you look through me. I can't stand it and that's what you did last time. You wanted to pretend it didn't happen. I can't. I get that you need boundaries, but I can't make love to you tonight and have you look through me in the morning."

What had she done to him? It was hard to remember that underneath that gorgeous exterior was a man with a man's feelings. She reached out and cupped his face, touching the scruff of his beard. "I won't ever look through you. I thought I could handle a one-night stand, but I didn't like how it made me feel either. I was scared. I still am. I don't know that this can work, but I'm willing to try. Let's change our boundaries a little bit. You can be my boss when we get to work, but we're friends and lovers until we walk in that door."

She wasn't fooling herself. They would still be friends and lovers, but she needed the small wall between them at work.

"And you'll let me take you home? I hate not seeing you home after work. I worry about you."

This was what Kai meant. Talk. Negotiations. They'd been wrong not to do it that first night, but she hadn't taken Javier seriously.

She hadn't taken herself seriously either. She'd accepted immediately that he wouldn't want her for more than a night. Why had she done that? Why had she expected that he would walk away?

Because that was what people did. They walked away when times got tough. Her father had. Her mother hadn't walked away exactly, but the minute she'd become troublesome, her mother had dismissed her. Kevin had his light-bulb moment shortly after she lost her arm.

So if she knew how it would end, did that mean she couldn't enjoy the parts in between? If she guarded herself, looked at the relationship realistically, she could keep him for as long as possible and then let him go when the time came.

Rules. Boundaries. As long as she respected them, she could do this.

"Yes, I'll let you drive me home." It was silly for them to take two cars.

He moved between her legs, bringing her closer to him. "I want one night a week where we do something together. One night is my choice."

That didn't seem fair. If he thought he was going to get her to go to basketball games or action flicks without any payback, he needed to figure out who he was playing with. "Fine. One night is my choice."

He smiled down at her. "All right. And one night a week we play."

And just like that she'd agreed to spend three of seven days with him. So dangerous, but she couldn't back away. Not when he was this close. Not when she could feel the heat coming off his body. He was a drug and she was definitely at risk of becoming addicted to him.

His mouth came down and she wasn't thinking about being reasonable anymore. His tongue tangled with hers and all those pesky thoughts floated away.

"We're not in your apartment, Jules. I don't want to play this vanilla." One hand fisted in her hair, gently drawing her head back. "Do you understand what I'm saying?"

Since he'd been using electricity to get her motor running, she thought they'd passed vanilla a long time ago, but she knew what he meant. "You want to be in charge."

"I am in charge of this and you want me to be."

"Yes." She was starting to crave this part of him. The happy, playful Javier was easy to be around, but the Dom inside made her ache to submit. The Dom reminded her there was much more to this man than good looks and a laid-back nature. "I want you in charge. I want to try this thing with you. I loved the way we were that night, but I think this could be even better. I liked sex, but I didn't need it the way I seem to with you."

"Because you didn't get what you need from other partners," he replied. "You liked the wand. You liked how it made you feel."

He was forcing her to look him in the eyes, to be honest with him. "Yes, I liked it. I liked how out of control I was, but I wouldn't have liked it with someone I didn't trust. I liked how it hurt at first, and then something seemed to open up inside me."

"Then trust me now." He released his hold on her hair. "Get up, turn around, and rest your torso on the table. I want those legs spread wide."

He helped her down and she turned around. It was awkward because she couldn't ease down gracefully with only one hand.

"Don't start in with the insecurities," he ordered. "If you need help, I'll help, but there's no room for your insecurities here."

She flopped down and spread her legs. It was weird and awkward, but she was tired of being worried about it. If Javier didn't care, why should she? She was sure some other sub would hold herself off the table, showing off the lean, elegant lines of her body. If Javier wanted elegant, he would be with someone else. It was time to stop doubting the man and start accepting that his actions matched his words.

"Better." His hand came down on her back. "See, I didn't get to spend enough time on this pretty ass the other night. That's the problem with vanilla hookup sex. Too often it's fast and furious. It's nothing more than a way to get off and quickly."

"Is that how it was with your previous women? The broom closet ones, not the subs." She didn't like to think about how many of them there had been.

His hand eased down her spine toward her backside. What was he doing? She tried to turn, to see him.

"Eyes forward." He said it with a smack to her ass.

She bit back a shout but turned her eyes to the wall. She didn't need to see. It was obvious this was his spanky time. It was her time to see if this did something for her.

Another slap to her ass, this time the other cheek. "There wasn't a lot of intimacy in the hookups, and for a very long time, that was the only kind of sex I had." Another smack, this one more serious. "I was working my ass off and I didn't have time for relationships or dating. I made it plain to every woman who was interested in me that a hookup was all they would get. And as for the subs, well, you're the first."

Three more smacks. Warmth spread through her, her skin seeming to come alive. "I thought you've been through training. How can I be the first?"

Two more slaps and then his hand slid between her legs, finding her pussy. "I trained plenty, and let me tell you Big Tag doesn't go easy on Doms. My training partner was a very nice lady named Mia who is now married to one of Big Tag's brothers. We were friends. No sex. After Mia, my brother came home and I tried to help out at his place for a while. I would play after work on Saturdays, but again, I didn't have any real time to spend on a woman, so I kept things light. The deepest relationship I had was the very cautious one I'd started with Kristy, and you saw how that worked out. I didn't even spend a whole night with her." His voice deepened. "You are soaking wet."

"Yes, I like the spanking thing." She also liked his hand on her flesh.

"This isn't a disciplinary spanking. This is meant to get you hot, and I'm happy to see it works. But I know something else that works, too."

She heard the sound of his jeans being unzipped, of a wrapper opening. She gripped the table, trying to balance herself.

"Let go. I told you. I'm in charge of this." He flipped her over the minute she obeyed.

He'd gotten naked at some point, and damn but she would never get used to the sight of his muscular body. She let her eyes drift down. His cock was long and thick, already encased in the condom. He moved her easily, settling her on the edge of the table.

She could feel where he'd spanked her, where he held her just on the edge. If he stepped away she would fall, but that was part of the intimacy. He wouldn't allow her to fall. She could play in dangerous waters because he wouldn't hurt her.

"Hold on to me. Only me." He started to rub against her, easing his dick inside.

She wrapped her arms around him, his body the only balance she had. He looked down, watching the place where his cock was disappearing inside her body.

"Take me," he commanded. "Take all of me."

He thrust inside, the sensation flaring through her. She was stretched in the best way. His cock invaded and dominated. Jules held on as Javier took over. He picked her up, impaling her on his cock.

He moved her up and down, showing off just how strong he was. She felt like she weighed nothing at all, like she was delicate and petite when she knew she was neither. She let her head fall back as he hit her sweet spot and the world seemed to explode all around her.

Javier moved her back to the table, setting her down before grinding out his own orgasm. He held her hard against him as he found his pleasure, kissing her over and over again.

He wrapped his arms around her when he was finished, giving her the intimacy she needed. "I didn't mean to do that, but damn I'm glad we did. I know we need to take this slow, but I don't think I'll be able to keep my hands off you when we play."

She smiled up at him. "I don't want you to, Sir. I like having your hands on me."

And she was already bargaining. She was already wondering what it would really hurt if he took her home and they spent the night together.

There was a knock on the door that had her clutching at him.

"Guys, I'm sorry to interrupt you," Eric said, opening the door. If he was shocked, she couldn't tell. There was a grave look on his face. "Javier, Derek Brighton just called. There was a break-in at your place. Your brother was injured. Apparently they were minor injuries, but they still need you back in Dallas."

Javier's face went blank and then he stepped back. "I'm sorry, Jules. I have to go."

Eric closed the door, leaving them alone again.

Jules reached out for him, but he was pulling his jeans off the floor. "I'll go with you. I can be ready to go in a few minutes."

"Absolutely not." He pulled the condom off, tied it, and tossed it in the handy trashcan. "I have no idea what I'm walking into."

"All the more reason for me to go with you." She hated the thought of him driving back to Dallas alone with no one to distract him.

"No," he said. "You stay here with Kai and Kori. They'll take you home."

"I thought you wanted to take me home." She hopped down and reached for her corset.

He stopped at the door. "I want you safe. Don't forget. You're the one who needs boundaries. We have to respect them. Let me handle this."

He walked out, leaving her alone and wondering if those boundaries were really what she needed after all.

Chapter Seven

Javier noticed the woman standing in the hall as he hurried toward his own apartment. She was dressed in a black trench coat, wearing a scarf with sunglasses over her eyes despite the lateness of the evening.

His stomach was in knots over his brother, but he didn't like the idea of some strange woman hanging around Jules's apartment. "Hello?"

She started to turn.

Derek Brighton stepped out of Javi's apartment. "Hey, I'm sorry we had to disrupt your evening."

Javier stopped in front of him. "What happened?"

"Come on in and we'll talk. The officer who handled the 911 call has already taken his report and I let him go. The EMTs offered to take Rafe to the ER but he refused."

Well, naturally he refused. His brother hadn't met a good idea he didn't refuse.

Javier glanced down the hall, but the woman was gone. He followed Derek inside and caught his first glimpse of his brother. Rafe was sitting in his chair, his face sporting a few bandages.

"What the hell happened? And where's the nurse? Is she okay?" He'd been trying to get information about the young woman who'd shown up to take care of Rafe, but no one seemed to know anything.

"According to your brother, she quit two hours in and left long before the problems started," Derek explained.

He turned to his brother. "She quit? She just started today. I find it hard to believe that she quit."

Rafe shook his head. "She was a bitch."

He felt his hands fist at his sides. "She was a young woman with excellent experience and credentials. What did you do? Because there's no doubt in my mind that this was all about you."

Rafe's red-rimmed eyes came up. "I don't need a keeper."

"So you fired her?" He was going to beat his brother way better than the others had. They hadn't gotten the job done right.

"I told you I don't need a fucking babysitter," Rafe growled. "I want to be alone."

"You can't be alone. You can barely get to the bathroom on your own right now," he argued. "You had surgery and you won't do the work it takes to walk again. Believe me, the minute you can get your own place to live, I'll be more than happy to let the door hit your ass."

"Oh, show me the way, brother," Rafe replied with a nasty tone. "I don't want to be here any more than you want me here."

Derek held up a hand. "Could you two stop for a second? I need to know what happened tonight."

Rafe shrugged. "I sent the nurse home and about an hour later, some guys broke in. I guess I didn't lock the door after the nurse walked out. I already explained all of this. I told the officer what happened."

"But you didn't give me a reason for the attack. Two guys showed up and beat the hell out of you, but they didn't take anything? They didn't give you a reason for hurting you?" There was pure suspicion in Derek's tone. "That doesn't happen. People don't randomly beat each other up."

"You never been in a bar at two in the morning?" Rafe asked.

"Even then someone has usually done something or said something to push the assailant to break," Derek explained. "According to you, you've never seen the two men before and they didn't say anything, merely walked in and beat the crap out of you."

Put like that, it didn't make a lot of sense. "Why would someone come here to beat you up, Rafe? Come on. You have to know something."

His brother's eyes came up. "Fine. You gonna push me? I didn't want to say this, but they weren't looking for me."

Javier's stomach turned. "What do you mean?"

Rafe shrugged. "I don't know who they were. I never saw them before. They came to the door and said they knew you and I let them in. I swear, brother, I wouldn't have called the damn police at all. I don't want to get you in some kind of trouble, but that busybody next door heard something and she called them in."

Someone was coming after him? This was about him and not Rafe? "What did they say?"

"Something about a woman." Rafe put a hand on his head. "I don't know. I was getting my ass kicked. I'm sure it was some husband whose wife you screwed. I told you that shit would come back to haunt you."

"I need a name," Javier tried. "Did they mention a woman's name?"

Rafe groaned. "I don't know. Something like Mary or Maria. I don't fucking know. Can you get out of my space, man? I'm tired. I want to go to bed, and yes, I can get myself into my own fucking bed."

He turned and wheeled himself out.

Javier stared after him. "That's my own fucking bed." He took a deep breath and turned back to Derek. Embarrassment flashed through him. His libido had always been a joke, but since he'd fallen for Jules, it had become something more. "I'm sorry you had to come out here."

Derek stood, his hand on his hips. "I'm not and I don't know that I buy his story."

"Story?"

The lieutenant stared at the door Rafe had disappeared behind. "I've been doing this for a very long time. I don't think he's telling the truth, Javier. He wouldn't look you straight in the eyes."

"He never does anymore. He hasn't since the accident." It was annoying. It was like his brother didn't want anyone to see what he was thinking, what was going on behind his eyes.

"It's more than that. Come down to the security office with me. I've got some questions about the tape," Derek said. "We've got a fairly decent view of at least one of the suspects. I want to see if you recognize him. The guy on duty has a couple of things to say, too."

Javier walked out with him, glancing down the hallway. No one was there. "Did you notice a woman hanging around Juliana's door?"

"Juliana?" Derek asked as they reached the elevator. He pushed the button to go down.

Derek hadn't been coming to Top as often as he had since he and his wife Karina had their baby. They'd moved out to the suburbs and the lieutenant hurried home after work. Since Jules hadn't been to Sanctum, they'd never met. "She's the new hostess at Top. She lives across the hall from me."

"Ah," he said as the elevator doors opened and they walked inside. "No, I didn't notice anyone, though when I got here there were a bunch of people in the hallway. Your neighbors are interesting. I had to explain to the lady down the hall that I was married. Apparently she's got single relatives."

"Yeah, that would be Mrs. Gleeson. I'm sure she's the one who called. She tends to know everything that goes on in this building." His brain was still whirling. "Derek, I have no idea who would come after me. I've calmed down a lot in the last year, and you know I wouldn't go after someone's wife. I can admit that I might not have always been so picky, but I've never had an actual affair with a married woman. Hell, I'm not proud of it, but most of my hookups don't even know my last name. How would their significant others even know where to find me?"

"Yeah, you shouldn't be proud of that," Derek agreed. "I assure you, if it was me and I wanted to slap you around a little, I could find you. But like I said, I'm not sure I buy that this attack was about you. Why would some upset husband beat on your wheelchair-bound brother? I would assume Rafe explained to the attackers that he wasn't you. Given the fact that this was supposedly all about some crazy, kinky sex, these gentlemen should have been able to put two and two together and figure out Rafe likely isn't chasing down married women for thrills."

"Or they decided to hurt someone I care about. I know I'm upset with him now, but he's still my brother. Maybe this guy decided that I'd taken something from him so he would hurt me, too." The thought scared the shit out of him. Would they come after Jules? Would whoever these assholes were try to hurt her?

The doors opened again and they walked out onto the first floor. Derek seemed to know his way around. He went immediately for the manager's office.

"Without leaving you a very specific threat? I doubt that. Men who are pissed that you slept with their wife tend to want you to know who's kicking your ass," Derek said. "Besides, you had that break-in last week. There were no other break-ins reported for the building. I think the two are connected."

"You think it's possible they've already sent me a message?" He'd been at Jules's apartment or they would have found him there. Would they figure out he had a woman and take it out on her?

Derek stopped at the office and knocked twice before opening the door. "I think they were sending someone a message. Sometimes these people speak in their own code, and unless you're on the inside, you wouldn't have any idea a message had been sent at all. Hey, Harold. Thanks for staying up. You have that video for me?"

Harold was the night security guard, though he was really more of the night super. He was an older man who was excellent at fixing a clogged pipe, but the thin man wasn't going to scare anyone off. They'd given him a Taser and called him a guard. The good news was he slept through most of his shift.

Harold yawned and pointed to the monitor. "Got it right here. I made a tape for your officer, too. Just press that button. Been a busy night."

It had been an amazing night right up to the point where it had all imploded.

Javier sat down, looking at the bank of monitors that took video of what went on in the hallways and the outer doors of the complex. When they were working.

"I backed it up a little," Harold explained before he touched the button to start the tape.

The time stamp was ten p.m. The hallway looked quiet, but he watched as Mrs. Gleeson stepped out, looking right and then left before she locked her door behind her. She put her keys in the pocket of her gown. There was a bottle of something in her hand.

"Is that wine?" Derek asked.

Oh, that wasn't a wine bottle. "Nope, I think Mrs. Gleeson's poison of choice this evening is whiskey. Holy shit. She's going to Mr. Cassidy's? I thought they hated each other."

Mr. Cassidy's door opened and a look of pure joy hit his face as he let the woman in. He even tapped her ass as she strolled through the door.

Those two liars. He was so going to blow that up. Or maybe not. It was good to have some golden years sex and scandals.

"So she wasn't next door?" That was the confusing part. The walls could be thin, but he knew he couldn't hear what was going on across the hall.

"Wait for it," Derek murmured.

As soon as Mr. Cassidy's door closed, the elevator opened and two men walked down the hall, straight to Javier's apartment.

Derek froze the frame just as one of the two men looked up. "Do you recognize him, Javi?"

Dark hair and eyes. Probably tall, muscular. "He looks somewhat familiar, but I can't recall his name. I might be wrong about it, too. I'm sorry. I wish I could tell you something more."

Both men were wearing dark hoodies. One of them knocked and Javier watched as Rafe opened the door. From the camera angle, he couldn't see Rafe past the moment when he'd greeted the men. He wheeled back and the door closed.

Javier shook his head. "I'm sorry. Maybe if I think about it for a while, I can come up with a name."

"I don't think you can." Derek pressed the fast-forward button.

After a long while, he stopped the tape again as the door opened and the two men left.

12:36 a.m.

What the hell? "They didn't beat on him for two hours. He wasn't that hurt."

"Yes," Derek said. "That was my assessment as well."

He saw Mrs. Gleeson open the door and she and her undercover lover watch the men leave. When they were far enough down the hall, she rushed over to her apartment.

"We got her 911 call four minutes later. I assume Rafe cried out or something and that's what got her ousted from her love shack," Derek said with a grin.

They'd been in his apartment for hours. What the hell had they been talking about because Derek was right. Rafe wasn't hurt enough for hours of torture. Someone had smacked him a couple of times, blackened his left eye, but that wouldn't take hours.

What the hell kind of trouble was his brother in?

To his left, he caught sight of what was going on at the front of the building. A familiar figure moved into the inner doors. Jules was standing there and she turned and waved at whoever was just out of camera range.

Kai and Kori had dropped her off.

He should be with her. He should run to the front doors and beg her forgiveness for leaving abruptly. He should tell her what was going on.

He should tell her he couldn't be with her until whatever was happening with Rafe got sorted out.

"Yeah, between those two and that high-and-mighty lady come looking for the new girl, it's been an exciting night," Harold was saying with a nod.

That got Javier's attention. "New girl? The one across the hall from me?"

Harold nodded. "Yeah, the one on 4." He shook his white head and whistled. "The fourth floor is the horny floor. Lots of people slipping into each other's places after hours."

Apparently. "Who was looking for Jules?"

Derek turned to him. "You said you saw someone hanging out around her door, right? She's got to be on camera."

"She was wearing sunglasses and a scarf." Was that woman a part of whatever the hell was happening? If this whole thing was about Rafe, why would anyone come after Jules?

Except if Rafe owed people money, some criminal elements would come after his family and friends if they thought it would work. Some wouldn't care that they were bringing in an innocent woman as long as they got what they wanted.

"She showed up and demanded to know where Juliana O'Neil was," Harold explained. "Never even took off those sunglasses. Very snobby, that one. I even offered her some ramen and she turned that nose of hers up and left in a snit. I'm getting too old for this job."

"Try to talk to your brother," Derek said, patting him on the shoulder in a sympathetic gesture. "This will go so much easier if he'll tell us the truth. I can't promise those assholes won't be back. Unless they got what they wanted, they very likely will, and your security here is…it's not the greatest."

"Nope," Harold agreed. "It's me and I'm usually napping. I told them I wasn't right for this job."

It was good to know everyone agreed.

Javier watched Jules as she made it to the fourth floor. She stopped at his place and he watched as she thought about knocking. Finally, she simply put her hand on his door and sighed before making her way to her own apartment, her shoulders slumped.

"Oh, is that the way it is?" Derek asked, that sympathy creeping into his tone.

"I have to keep her safe."

"Yes, but be careful how you do it," Derek offered. "If you care about this woman, be honest with her. Don't pull the martyr thing or it won't go well. I'll work this from my end and see if we can figure it out as quickly as possible. You take care of your lady."

He was beginning to wonder if *he* was the problem in his lady's life.

Chapter Eight

Jules walked toward the kitchen, adjusting her black dress. It was concert night and Top had been transformed. The small stage in the bar had been expanded and there were already record company people in the front of house, taking pictures and changing what they didn't like.

They treated her and the serving staff a lot like interns, ordering them all around and not caring that they had other things to do. Yes, Jules remembered this particular work style. She preferred Top, where everyone respected their fellow coworkers. Not so in her mother's world. There was a hierarchy and it must be followed.

Not that this was precisely her mother's world, but it was close enough.

Of course, everyone wasn't an asshole. She'd been introduced to the singer they were featuring this evening. Her name was Emily Young and she'd been kind and very accommodating to the entire staff. Blonde and tiny and gorgeous. She was in the early stages of her career, having been plucked from a bar by one of country music's hottest male singers, Luke Berry. The record company was sending her on tour and one of the ways they intended to roll her out was giving her small, exclusive venues to play. Tonight, Top was only open to a select crowd who would enjoy dinner service and then the concert.

Jules moved past the last of the tables, unable to get her mind off the singer. Emily Young had her whole life ahead of her, her dreams just starting to come true. What must that feel like? At her age, Jules had known she wanted to cook, but hadn't known how she wanted to do it. There had seemed to be one and only one path ahead of her, and the expectation had been enormous.

Now that she was settled and knew exactly what she wanted, the choice had been taken away from her.

"Exciting night, huh?" a familiar voice asked.

Jules looked down and there was Suzanne. The petite brunette had a menu in front of her despite the fact that the evening's menu was fixed.

Jules gave Suzanne a polite smile. "Yes, it is. Are you with the record company or the network?"

"Aren't they all one and the same these days? The network Chef Taggart sometimes works for is owned by the record company that recently discovered the sweet and talented Emily Young, straight out of Bell Buckle, Tennessee. Isn't it funny the ties we all have? We forget how small the world is and how easy it is for our lives to cross over and entwine."

"Yes, it is." Her mother worked for that network, though Jules hardly thought Annaliese O'Neil would care that a tiny restaurant in Dallas was hosting a singer for the night. "I hope you enjoy the show."

"How are things with you and the handsome sous chef?" Suzanne asked, leaning forward. "I've been out of town for a bit, but I missed this place." Her eyes trailed over to the bar.

Was she staring at the bodyguard? Declan Burke was going over some protocols with his fellow security for the evening. Now that she thought about it, the brunette only seemed to show up on nights when the bodyguard was here.

She felt for the man. Apparently he was having issues with

cluster headaches. She'd found him lying across a table earlier, a cold cloth on his face. Now he looked like nothing was wrong, but there was a tightness to his eyes that made her wonder.

"We work quite well together," Jules said with what she hoped was a content tone. She didn't want to get into her fucked-up love life with a virtual stranger, but she also didn't want to be rude to a customer.

Suzanne's smile dimmed. "Oh, well. It's good to have a nice working relationship. Please tell the staff that it all smells delicious. I'm looking forward to the evening."

Something about the way she'd lost that high-wattage smile made Jules stop. Why would the woman be disappointed? She didn't know Jules or Javier, but Jules could see plainly her answer bugged the lady.

"Can I ask why you're interested?" She put the question in a soft tone, not wanting to offend, but her curiosity got the better of her.

"Isn't everyone interested in love?" Suzanne asked wistfully. "I suppose not. Like I told you before, I consider myself a decent matchmaker. I would have put you with him in a heartbeat. You mesh quite well. That's the key to a good pairing. Each partner lifts the other up. Your weaknesses would be bolstered by his strengths, and vice versa. Perhaps you're not ready."

"Perhaps he's not ready," Jules shot back, though she'd thought the same thing the day before. She wasn't even sure why she was talking, but it seemed to come naturally around the brunette. "I thought we had an agreement but he almost immediately changed it. I think he wants me if I'm convenient."

"Oh. That's not good at all," Suzanne said with a shake of her head. "It makes me sad. He struck me as a man who would be willing to go far for a woman he cared about. You know the type. They treat all women alike until they find the right one. So the first time you gave him trouble he dumped you?"

"No. He didn't dump me. Not yet. I'm afraid he's about to." She'd understood why he'd left her the night before, but this morning had the definite feel of a brush-off to her. She'd called him and asked if they could go to breakfast. His phone had gone to voice mail. Instead of calling back, he'd told her via text he had to come into work early and he'd see her there.

Suzanne waved a hand and Jules got another look at the mark on her wrist. A single quarter-sized round mark that had to be a brand. What was that about? "That sounds like pessimism. No one ever got what they wanted by thinking it wouldn't happen. You should go in there and find out what he's afraid of. Men do silly things when they're afraid. Women, too. Foolish things they think they can't take back. I've found the key to it all is to have a little faith. Nothing is taken without something being given back."

Jules held up her prosthetic, letting go of her curiosity about the mark. "You'll forgive me if I disagree. Well, I guess they gave me this plastic thing. Not a good trade-off in my eyes."

"No, you're not looking at it in the proper fashion. You were given a challenge, Juliana," Suzanne said quietly. "That's something a lot of people don't get. The ones like you, the ones given a great challenge to overcome, get to truly find out what they're made of. It's a harsh lesson at times, but how good it must be to know that you can face it all. How confident a woman that must make you. That's the gift."

The gift? There had been pain and loss. No gift. She certainly wasn't more confident.

"Tell me something, Juliana," Suzanne said. "How are the recipes coming? The ones from your grandmother's book."

The words startled her for a moment. "How did you know about that?"

"You mentioned it a while back," Suzanne replied with a smooth smile. "You said you were trying to make the recipes easier to deal with because you missed them. You wanted to substitute in easier to deal with ingredients."

For the life of her, she couldn't remember that conversation, but then sometimes dinner service was a whirl of activity. All the time, really. "Uhm, it's not going well, actually. Everything I try seems a little off. I guess my grandmother knew what she was doing. I'll miss those foods."

"Why?"

"I can't cook the way I used to."

Suzanne laughed brightly and waved her hand. "Oh, is that all? Well, then you'll find another way to cook, won't you?" She stood up. "Never give up on your dreams. We're lost when we give up. I think I'll go introduce myself to Ms. Young. I suspect she's not one to give up on her dreams, either, though I believe she left something behind in that hometown of hers. Well, I suspect he'll show up eventually. All the good ones do."

She watched as the singer greeted Suzanne like an old friend.

Jules turned to walk away as the door to the kitchen opened and Javier stuck his head out.

"Good, you're here. I need you," he said briskly.

She followed after him, the odd conversation with Suzanne playing through her head. There wasn't time to think about it now, though.

Except she couldn't help but think about the part where she was inconvenient. She'd been inconvenient for most of the time she'd known Javier. She'd kind of driven him crazy. He was in a bad place with his brother. She should give him some space.

Or she should figure out what her real place with him was.

The kitchen buzzed all around her, every station hopping with action, and the sweet smell of barbecue permeated the air.

"Can we talk for a minute?" Jules asked. "You never got back to me about what happened last night. Is Rafe all right?"

He stopped and turned to her, his expression softening. "I'm sorry about this morning. And last night. I got busy and I didn't call you. That was wrong of me."

At least he wasn't pushing her away. "What happened?"

He moved to one of the stations that wasn't being used. "There was another break-in. I told you about how the night of the blackout someone broke in and messed my place up. Well, it happened again. Sweetheart, Rafe is in trouble. I don't know what kind of trouble yet, but some guys hurt him last night."

So much shifted and slipped into place. She'd been around Rafe enough to suspect a few things about him, but she hadn't talked to Javier because she wasn't sure how he would take it. Now she couldn't hold back. All the secrecy, the bouts of anger and depression, the refusal to even try to walk…it added up in her mind.

"Check his pain meds." She hated the fact that she had to tell him this, but she'd been thinking about it a lot. "He's far enough out from the original injury that he shouldn't need the strong stuff."

Javier's face went blank. "He recently had surgery."

"And I bet he's taking more than the prescribed amount. Javier, I know he's your brother and you love him, but I've seen this happen a lot," she replied. "Those drugs are habit forming if you don't carefully watch your intake. It's best to get off them as soon as you possibly can function without them."

"He's not a drug addict." Javier's arms crossed over his chest.

Damn it, she shouldn't have said anything, but she couldn't stop now. She understood what he was trying to do, but Rafe's choices were putting Javier in danger. His place had been broken into twice, and if Rafe couldn't handle his bills, they would come after Javier. "You have to confront him about it. He'll lie to you, but you can get him to admit it. That's the first step."

"He doesn't need steps," Javier said stubbornly.

"Babying him isn't going to help." She'd seen too many good men and women go wrong because their family wouldn't accept what the problem was. She got it. She did. It was hard to send a child/sibling/parent off to war only to have them come home to face something even worse than losing a limb.

"Babying him?" Javier practically shouted the question. "How the fuck can you say that? He lost both his legs."

She lowered her tone. "A lot of people lost pieces of themselves. Sebastian lost both legs, too. How long was it before he was walking? Rafe should be walking by now. He isn't because he doesn't want to, likely because he's addicted to his pain meds and they dull every single sense he has."

He frowned at her. "You don't know him. Rafe wouldn't do

that."

"You know he's been abusing alcohol," she pointed out. She wasn't sure why he was being so resistant. It was obvious to her Rafe needed help, and it wouldn't come in the form of pretending everything was okay. "How is this different? And it explains why you've had bad dudes at your apartment. They were looking for money or product."

His jaw went tight. "Like I said, you don't know anything about my brother. He wouldn't do that to me. Now, on to the reason I called you back here. I need someone cutting veg. Use the new cutting board and I'll get you a proper knife. I need a medium chop on those onions."

She stopped, surprised at the command coming from him. And the nature of the command. She glanced at the cutting board like it was a snake that would bite her if she let it. "I'm the hostess, Javier. Or have you forgotten that? I don't work in the kitchen."

"Drake has the flu and Ben's father had a heart attack. Chef gave him the night off. I had to shift everyone around. I need my line chefs working on the dishes," he said brusquely. "You're the only one with experience."

She shook her head. "I can't."

Javier's dark eyes narrowed. "Are you telling me you don't know how to? Because you're a trained cook. You might not have graduated from a famous culinary academy, but you're trying to tell me your mother didn't even teach you knife skills?"

"I did her *mis en place* for years. Of course I know how to dice an onion," she replied tightly, well aware every eye was on them.

"Then get to it. Like I said, I need a medium chop. It shouldn't be hard. I'm not asking for brunoise. I need that bag cut within the next…" He looked over to Jaylen's section. "How soon you need the onions?"

"I need to start in twenty, Chef," Jaylen replied with a sheepish look her way.

"You have twenty minutes." He turned to walk back to his station.

She reached out for him. "I can't, Javi. Have you noticed that this hand no longer works? It's not there so I can't use it."

"Then use your other hand, damn it. That one still works fine." He walked over to the cutting board. It had been sitting there for days, taunting her. He pulled out an onion and placed it on the board. He pointedly placed his right arm behind his back and used his left hand to cut the onion in two. Within seconds he had that sucker peeled and he placed it on the spikes to keep it still. He eased the chef knife sideways, cutting from the top to the bottom, and then brought it down from the outside in to dice.

He was fluid and graceful. He was quick. He'd done it all with one hand, and not his dominant one.

She felt her skin flush with embarrassment. "How long did you practice that? Trying to show up the new chef? Or is this performance all for me?"

He stared at her, a look that could have frozen water. "This is about you wasting your talent smiling at people and making sure they know where to sit. You've worked in kitchens all your life. You know that everyone throws in when we need it. Are you going to do what I asked or should I call Ally in here? She doesn't have your experience, but she knows how to fucking try."

"I'll get her." And then she just might walk out of here. He was an asshole and she should have seen it from the beginning.

"So I shouldn't baby Rafe, but it's okay to baby you," he said, his voice low.

She turned on him. "I was unaware you were babying me at all."

His eyes closed briefly. "Jules, this is stupid. You can do this. You're trying to find any way to make your life happen except to do the actual work you need to do to be who you want to be."

The actual work had been thousands of hours spent toiling beside her mother, learning knife techniques when she was a kid. She'd given half her life to this fucking profession and it was all blown to hell because she'd needed to get away from her mom, to prove to herself that she could be independent. The last thing she needed was some man to tell her what to do.

151

Not only had Javier been manipulating her, he'd put her on display, berating her in front of everyone.

Of course, she'd also told him his brother was an addict in front of everyone. Maybe he thought it was good payback.

"Fuck you, Javier." She turned and walked out.

And immediately ran into Chef. Sean Taggart was standing there, leading someone into the kitchen.

From the looks on their faces, they'd heard everything.

Jules stared at the woman she'd been fairly certain she wouldn't see again. "Hi, Mom."

Chapter Nine

Javier watched her walk away and felt a pit open in his gut.

What the hell had he done? Why had he pushed her like that?

He glanced around and everyone was suddenly very interested in the work in front of them. Their heads were down, the perfect image of professionals, but they'd all witnessed what he'd done to her.

It wasn't what he'd meant to do. He'd meant to play a long game. He'd brought in the cutting board. It was the first step. If he could get her interested in practicing the basics, she would figure out that she wasn't as limited as she thought she was.

And then she'd stood there and told him he was babying Rafe. The accusation had rankled especially because he knew damn well he was babying her.

Fuck.

He had to talk to her. He started out the door but was stopped when Chef walked in.

"Excuse me," Javier said, ready to walk around him.

Sean put a hand out. "Are you going after Jules? You the one who put that look on her face?"

Shit. Sean could be super protective of the women who worked for him. The men, too, but that came out in another way. When it came to a woman Sean felt a responsibility to, he could get downright mean. But he needed to understand that Jules was Javier's responsibility and she was going to stay that way.

Unless she told him to fuck off and left town. Which she might after what he'd done to her.

"We had a disagreement. I gave her a direct order and she didn't take it well," he admitted.

One brow rose over Sean's eyes. "You did? Over the cutting board? I've been waiting for you to do that for days, man. You're not going to get her to try by easing her into it. She needs to be pushed into it. She's not a weak woman. Treat her like she's still in the military."

"I tried. It didn't go well."

Macon cleared his throat. "There were other things said. Things no commanding officer would say to his inferior."

Sean looked to the pastry chef. "Why do you know about it?"

"Because they threw down in front of the entire kitchen," Macon admitted. "And it was a pretty spectacular fight. When she said she couldn't do it, Javier showed her up. Put one hand behind his back and proved he could."

Sean winced. "No wonder she looked like that. Well, you can't go after her now. She's had some unexpected company. It looks like the network sent out special invites to some of the bigwigs to tonight's performance. Guess who took them up on it?"

He was confused for a moment and then a few things fell into place. The woman at Jules's apartment had been looking for her, but not for nefarious reasons. "Her mother."

"Yeah," Sean admitted. "I think Linc nearly had a heart attack. That kid likes decorating way too much. How did he survive Army barracks? Anyway, she's out there and I have Jules setting her up. Your fight's going to have to wait. We've got less than an hour before the rest of the invitees show up. I need everyone focused. Where are we on the meatball sliders?"

Jaylen held a hand up. "Uhm, I kind of need those onions."

Fucking onions. "I'll cut them myself. I tried to get Jules to help out. It did not go well."

"Apparently you were an ass," Sean said. "If it helps, you were always going to have to be an ass about this. She needs the push. Face it, man. This is what it means to be in a relationship."

"I'm not very good at it." He had a sinking feeling. "Maybe I should go back to broom closet hookups. They don't need anything from me. It's a lot easier."

He didn't seem to be good at any of it. He was fucking up with Rafe. He'd just broken something inside Jules, and it hadn't been his intention. Not at all.

She'd said something about not being ready for a relationship. Maybe he was the one who wasn't ready. Maybe he never would be.

Sean sighed. "It might be easier, but empty hookups aren't what will make your life worthwhile. I'll go and ask Ally or Tiffany to help with prep. That said, our guest would like to introduce herself."

He opened the kitchen door and a petite blonde dressed in a beautiful yellow sundress and cowboy boots walked in.

Every guy in the place perked up because that was one gorgeous woman. She had a bright smile and mischievous eyes, as though she knew her place in the world and sat back and enjoyed the ride. She was exactly the type of woman he would have tried to spend a little time with before.

And he couldn't work up the will to smile at her because she wasn't Juliana.

"Hi, everyone. I'm Emily Young and I'm going to be coming through town again in a few months with Luke Berry and I can't thank you enough for hosting this little warm-up session for me. Everything smells like heaven. I can't wait for supper, but I wanted to come back here and beg you to please come out and enjoy the show. I know you all have work to do, but I need a real audience, if you know what I mean. I can't think of anyone I would like to perform for more than a bunch of American heroes who served our country proudly and who also happen to know how to cook. Chef Taggart, do you hire any men who aren't incredibly hot?"

That had every man in the place chuckling. He would hand it to her. She was charming as hell.

So why was he stuck on a sarcastic, introvert of a woman who couldn't see that she was holding herself back? Why did it have to be Jules?

"You know, my wife does a lot of the hiring," Sean was saying. "I would say she has a type." He clapped his hands. "So let's get working. Don't let the lady down."

As Emily made her way around the kitchen introducing herself and asking tons of questions, Javier found Ally and they started the prep. Every time he looked up from his station, he wanted to see Jules there, glimpsing over and smiling at him, working with him, challenging him.

It couldn't work if she wouldn't try.

It couldn't work if he wouldn't face the fact that Rafe had a serious problem. He needed to focus on his brother. If he went out there and found Jules, he would do nothing but bring her into his hell, and she'd been through enough of that.

He went back to his dish, wondering all the while if it wouldn't be better to let her go.

Two hours later, Javier watched Jules across the room. Emily launched into another song, her lovely voice filling the space with emotion.

Fucking emotions. He was having a million of them.

They hadn't spoken through dinner service. Jules had come back into the kitchen a few times, helping Ally and Tiffany, but she hadn't once looked at him. She stood at the back of the small crowd, across the restaurant from him, as though she was going to try to keep as much space between them as possible.

He glanced over to one of the tables nearer to the front. Annaliese O'Neil was seated there. She looked a lot like her daughter. Red haired and lovely and stubborn. Even listening to a country-western performance, the woman was sitting with perfect posture.

What the hell was he going to do about Jules?

"It's hard, you know," a deep voice said. Sebastian stood behind him. They were far enough back that with a low tone he wouldn't disrupt the performance. "It's hard to adjust to losing a piece of yourself. The world looks different than it did before. It can take time to decide to move forward."

"I don't think she wants to. I wouldn't have a problem with that, but I don't think she'll be happy. I think she's been running from this decision for a long time and she'll never be content with a man who's doing what she dreamed about," he whispered back.

He knew she wouldn't be happy on the sidelines of his world. He wanted to bring her in, to make her a partner. They could be a team. It would be one thing if she truly couldn't manage it. Then he would sit down and figure out something else that would fill her soul, but he knew in his heart that she could do this. She could have this part of herself back.

"If it helps at all, Tiffany agrees with you," Sebastian replied. "Tiffany says she talks about the dishes all the time, how it was cooked, what techniques were used. But you can't make Jules try. I can, however, promise you that if you step away from her tonight, she won't let you in again. I know because I would have done the same thing had Tiffany retreated."

He'd always thought the seemingly uptight sommelier and the bright, vivacious waitress made an odd couple, but they worked. Sebastian smiled more now and he'd eased up on having to look and act like nothing had ever happened to him. There were days when Tiffany would push him in his wheelchair. That would never have happened before their marriage.

"She's angry with me," Javier replied. "And honestly, it might be best if I took a step back. I don't know what's happening with my brother and it could be dangerous."

Except he did know. Deep inside he knew she was right. He simply didn't know what to do about it.

"Best for her? I don't know about that. I know that scene in the kitchen was bad, but at least she showed some emotion. You bring that out in her. No one else. I think if you leave her alone, she'll close off that part of herself and won't open it again. That would be a terrible shame." Sebastian stepped back and turned to his wife, holding out a hand as the music changed to a slow ballad. "Dance with me, love. I'm not very graceful, but I'll try for you."

Tiffany went straight in Sebastian's arms, swaying with her husband in the shadows.

And he knew that no matter what happened tomorrow, he couldn't leave Jules like this.

Emily Young's rich voice brought the crowd into her song.

Don't tell me it's too late...

He moved around the crowd, catching Juliana's stare. Her eyes flared as though she finally realized he was coming for her.

Don't call me darlin' and tell me you're leaving...

For a moment he thought she might run, but then there it was. The light of challenge. Her shoulders squared and she stepped away from the crowd, obviously ready to do battle.

Was Sebastian right? Would she fight with anyone else? Or would she treat all the others like she did life itself—something to amuse her but nothing serious.

Don't walk away...

"Javier," she began.

He shook his head. "No. No fighting. No talking. Dance with me. Just be with me for a few minutes. I don't know what's going to happen tomorrow. I only know that I've never loved anyone the way I love you."

He might only have a chance to say it once. She might not forgive him. God only knew what would happen with Rafael. But they had this moment and he had to say it because he wasn't ever going to say it to another woman.

Stop pushing me when you know you want to hold on...

For a second he thought she would walk away, and then she was in his arms. Jules wrapped her arms around him, holding on like she wouldn't, couldn't let go.

"I don't know what to do," she whispered.

His heart broke because that was their problem. He knew what to do, but she didn't, and that meant she wasn't ready. It was simple for him. She'd walked into his life and the world had become a brighter place. He merely confused her, unsettled her. He upset her carefully balanced life. He wasn't good for her.

He held on to her, knowing what he would do at the end of the song. He breathed her in, trying to memorize everything about this woman, his woman.

She would be his in his heart, in his dreams.

It could be so easy for us, baby. I've been here but you don't see me.

"Don't worry about it," he whispered. "You don't have to do anything. I'm going to step away at the end of this song and we're going to be friends, if you'll forgive me. I never meant to hurt you. I never meant to make things worse."

"I don't know what I want." The words came out of her mouth on a stifled cry. She buried her head in his shoulder.

He'd never seen her cry.

He'd done this to her.

Javier held on, hugging her tight and swaying for comfort more than to find the rhythm. He finally understood what his parents had. They'd loved each other, wanting the best for the other person far more than they'd ever wanted anything for themselves.

But it only worked if they were both in it. That was the hell of it all. Her distance lessened his love not one ounce.

"It's going to be okay," he promised her. "I won't ever hurt you again, sweetheart."

She cried into his shoulder as the song played on.

He prayed it would never end.

* * * *

Jules opened the back door, leading her mother past the kitchen and out into the evening. She tried not to look Javier's way. She couldn't.

Not when that dance had felt like good-bye.

When the song had ended, she'd run to the bathroom because she couldn't let her mother see her crying. She couldn't let anyone see her crying.

"So you work here, but not in the kitchen." Her mother sat down at one of the picnic tables behind the restaurant.

The employee break space consisted of a basketball net and two picnic tables so employees could escape during their breaks. It was a well-kept space, but more about function than form. It was a place where she'd started to feel comfortable.

After that incident with Javier, it might be a place she didn't see again. It rolled in her gut even as she tried her hardest to look calm. The fight was right there. Even after he'd held her and promised that everything would be okay, something had been left undone. It felt unfinished, but then she should never have started at all. She'd known it deep in her gut. She should have kept it to one night because she was never going to be happy as the significant other of a man who would live the dream that should have been hers.

God, had she just thought that? How selfish was she?

Was that really why she was holding herself apart from Javier? Why she hadn't told him the words that had been right there on her lips?

I love you.

He loved her and she held back. He'd actually said the words and she hadn't been able to return them to him. She'd known in that moment she might never be able to even though she felt them.

When had she become such a fucking coward?

Her mother looked incredibly out of place in her Chanel sheath and Louboutin heels. Her hair was perfectly done and didn't move even as the slight breeze blew through.

"Yes. I work here. I've been here for a couple of months. After I was discharged, I needed a job and one of Kevin's friends came through with this one. Chef pays well and there are other benefits." Ones she wouldn't use now since there was no way she would be playing anymore.

Why had he been cruel to her in the kitchen? She got that he'd been upset she'd called his brother an addict, but he'd obviously been planning that show of his for a while. He'd gotten excellent with his non-dominant hand, proving himself superior in every way. How long had it taken him? A week? Two? She kind of hated him for that, for how easy it came for him. He was a golden boy.

"Yes, I saw a documentary on this place," her mother said quietly. "I hear they offer a range of services for their employees. Chef Taggart is very interested in hiring veterans. He takes them in and teaches them how to cook. It's a worthy endeavor."

Something in her mom's tone didn't feel right to Jules. "Most of his recruits end up in culinary school. He takes the ones who show promise and he sends them to train. It's a real restaurant, not a charity."

"I know that. I didn't say it wasn't real." Her mother looked older, as though the few years they'd been apart were more like a decade. Makeup and lighting did wonders for her on television, but in the late evening light, Jules could see how her mother had aged.

"Why are you here, Mom?" She needed to get this over with so she could move on to the problem of finding another job and another apartment because she sure as hell wasn't going back to watching the women come and go out of Javi's love den. No matter what he'd said, if they weren't together, he would find someone else. That was how the world worked. Men loved women, but they didn't wait very long before finding another one to give them what they needed. He wouldn't be mean to her, but she couldn't handle it happening in front of her face.

"I wanted to see you and I needed an excuse, I suppose," her mother replied. "When I got the invitation from the network, I thought I couldn't put it off anymore. I've been talking to this woman, you see. Odd thing. She's the star of a niche Internet cooking show. "Angel in the Kitchen." You should watch it sometime. She's very telegenic. I'm trying to talk her into coming on the show. Suzanne. Lovely young woman."

Well, at least now she knew why Suzanne had hung around. She'd wanted an in. It shouldn't surprise her. "I'm glad you made a friend."

Her mother shook her perfectly coiffed head. "It's more than that. She made me think about you, about mistakes I've made. Sometimes we do things for reasons that seem right at the time. But what they're really about is fear and trying to stay in control of something I couldn't. I tried calling you."

She'd seen her mother's name on the screen and known she wasn't ready to deal with any of this. "You didn't leave messages. I thought it couldn't possibly be important."

Her mother turned to her. "I didn't know what to say."

"Hello. How's it going, Jules? Miss that hand much?" She'd noticed the one thing her mom hadn't stared at was her hand. She'd seemed fascinated with everything else about Jules, but not once had her mother's eyes gone to her missing hand.

"Stop with the sarcasm, Juliana. Please." She looked away, staring out into the alley. "I tried to go to your place last night. You weren't there."

"I was out." She'd been melting in Javier's arms. "I didn't get in until late."

"Do you have a new man in your life?"

That was easy. "No. I was out with friends. You know how it can be after work."

They worked hard and played hard. They kept late hours because they often didn't start work until the afternoon if they were on dinner service.

Her mother's lips curled up faintly, as though remembering some long-forgotten good time. "Yes, I suppose so. When I worked in your grandparents' diner, I would sometimes sneak in the back with one of the short-order cooks. He could have been your father, if you'd been lucky."

She felt her jaw drop. "Mother."

Her mom shrugged slyly. "Well, I did have a life and he was lovely. All I'm saying is I do understand and I'm happy you have friends. Why are you a hostess? Does this Taggart fellow not hire female chefs? I can make him, you know."

"I don't think he's had any apply," she shot back. The whole conversation made her sick. Her life revolved around this conversation. "I don't want to talk about my job. Why don't you tell me why you didn't bother to show up at my hospital bed? I would have thought at least you could have gotten a show out of it. I fully expected you to come barging in with a camera crew, but you never did. What's wrong? Do you not need the military demographic?"

Her mom seemed to shrink a bit in the face of her bitter words. "You changed your next of kin when you got married. Did you know the Navy didn't inform me when you were injured? I didn't know you were injured at all until much later."

She hadn't known? That thought had never once occurred to Jules. Her mother knew everything. Her mother had always seemed to have eyes everywhere because she couldn't stand to not know. How hard had it been to let go? To not know where her daughter was in the world for months and years at a time? "I thought Kevin told you."

"Kevin didn't call me for almost a month." Her mother's voice sounded ragged. "He kept that information from me for a month. I'm afraid he doesn't like me very much. I wasn't kind to him in the beginning, but then he was the enemy."

"He was a kid, Mom. Like I was a kid." Still, it felt good to know her mom hadn't ignored her. Kevin had known how angry she'd been with her mom. He'd likely thought he was helping out.

So many good intentions gone wrong because no one had talked it out. No one had sat and made things plain. Relationships of all kinds were worth the work of talking and negotiating.

Why did she walk away so easily?

"But you were my kid and he was taking you away," her mother said with a sigh. "In my mind, he was definitely the enemy."

Jules felt years away from that arrogant girl she'd been. "No, it wasn't Kevin's fault. I would have left anyway. I hated college and you wouldn't let me do what I wanted to do."

"Did it occur to you that there were other places you could work? That you could have fought me harder? You didn't have to throw away your future." The words came quickly out of her mom's mouth, as though she knew she had very little time to make her case.

She was right. Jules stood. "I think we're done here. We've had this argument before. You know, I thought you would be thrilled. I mean, I finally did it. I proved you right. I went out into the big bad world and I lost everything. You should get an *I told you so* T-shirt. You could sell it to your fans."

Her mother stood as well, blocking her path. "You think this is what I wanted? I spent my whole life working to protect you. I knew exactly what the big bad world could do to you. Why do you think I fought so hard? I worked day and night to pull us up out of the poverty your father left us in. Do you think I wanted you to have to slave away in kitchens? You were too smart for that."

"I fooled you, didn't I, Mom? And I didn't think working in kitchens was slaving away. I loved it. I loved every minute we spent in that first restaurant you opened. I would come in after school and wash dishes because I wanted to hang out. You think you built an empire for me, but all I ever wanted was that little Italian place on the square. I cried my eyes out when you sold it."

"You were fifteen, Juliana. You couldn't run it and I needed the cash for something bigger."

Jules held up her good hand. "I'm over that. I don't blame you. It was yours to sell, but I wasn't yours to keep. You didn't get to pick my future. You still don't. If you came here to get me back in college so I can count your cash, you wasted a first-class ticket."

"I came here to see my daughter," her mother yelled.

She'd never heard her mother yell. Not once. Not when her father left. Not when the bill collectors showed up. Not when the world had gone to hell. It was enough to make her stop.

Her mother seemed to flush and calm all at once, like an overfilled balloon that had finally popped. She leaned against the table. "I let the time slip by. I told myself you would be back. You would get out there and realize how terrible the world is and you would come home."

"I liked the Navy, Mom. I liked feeling like my life had some meaning. I liked helping people. Hell, I wouldn't change things. That's the crazy part. I wouldn't even go back and change it all.

Getting my arm back would mean five people died. I sacrificed."

She had. She'd sacrificed her arm. Did she have to sacrifice everything else? Did she sacrifice her dreams because they'd suddenly become harder to achieve?

Did she sacrifice her man because her pride meant more than he did?

Pride? Shouldn't she be proud? She'd survived. Shouldn't she try her hardest to thrive?

Her mother straightened up, coming to stand in front of her. "I prayed you would come home. I worried about you. But I never stopped loving you and I'm ashamed that I punished you for leaving me. I did it because I couldn't punish your father or your grandfather or all the other people along the way who left me alone. I did that to you because you hurt me."

Jules felt her heart break. "Oh, Mom, I didn't mean to. I just had to figure out who I am. I couldn't be a clone of you."

Her mom reached up, touching her for the first time in years. "Look at me and if you don't ever believe a word I say, you believe this: I am proud of you. I am so proud of you. Baby, if you want to stay here and find yourself, at least let me help. Let me upgrade your hand. They tell me it's not very high tech. Can I please do that? You think what I do is shallow, but it has meaning to me if I can I help my daughter."

If she upgraded her hand, she would likely be able to do more with it. Not everything. It wouldn't be perfect. She wouldn't be perfect. What was the point if she couldn't be...

If she couldn't be the perfect vision of who she'd been before, it wasn't worth even trying?

Adaptation. She hadn't been trying to adapt. She'd been trying to hide.

"I went into the water," she heard herself saying. "I did it knowing I could die, Mom. I didn't want to die. I just knew I couldn't live with myself if I didn't try to save them."

"Yes, my darling. That's why I'm begging you to forgive me. I was the weak one. I was scared and instead of talking it out with you,

I tried to control you. Instead of trying to understand, I punished you."

But it was her fault, too. She'd skipped her mom's calls, and slowly but surely the days had gotten away from her. It got easier and easier to sit back and make excuses for why she didn't have to try. She'd moved to Dallas because she'd known no one would look at her with sympathy and talk about the good old days when she'd had two hands.

What had Suzanne said? There was a gift in everything. That people who had gone through a trial knew who they were.

She'd been trying to find herself. She'd gone into that water a woman who didn't back down, who helped the people around her, who fought for what she wanted.

Because her mother had taught her never to back down.

She'd come out too afraid to even try in case she failed and proved her mother right.

"I'm sorry, Mom." Something opened inside her, some piece of her she'd thought long buried.

Her mother rushed in, hugging her tight. "No. I'm sorry. I love you, baby, and that means supporting you even when I think you're wrong. I've missed you, Juliana. I've missed you like I missed a piece of my soul."

She held her mother for the longest time and when they sat back down, they finally did what they should have done that day so long ago. They talked.

An hour later, she waved as her mom's limo rolled out. They'd said all the things they should have said and the deep breach between them had started to heal.

So why was she so fucking angry?

Why was the rage stirring inside her?

She sat back down, the moon high above offering illumination to the small space.

The door opened and Macon walked out, a trash bag over his shoulder. He stepped gingerly down the stairs, something he would likely do for the rest of his life because he only had one leg.

Yet there he was walking along because she was wrong. He had two legs. One was natural. One wasn't.

"Hey, Jules," Macon said, nodding her way. "I thought you'd left."

She spent all her time bemoaning her fate. Pretending that she wasn't bemoaning her fate, really. She played a damn good game. She put on a happy face and deflected all those pesky questions about what she would do with the rest of her life.

She said she wanted to find herself. Well, she was learning that sometimes that didn't happen in some fun, Hollywood, get-an-education, see-the-world-and-magically-land-where-you-should way.

No. Sometimes it happened with blood and sacrifice and loss. Sometimes the person we figured we were wasn't the one we wanted to be.

But she could change that. She could fight that. She'd never allowed her mother to choose who she would be, what she would be, and yet she was sitting here allowing a circumstance to do the very same thing. Put her in a box. But there was one thing she knew—boxes could be busted open.

"Jules, are you okay?"

She looked up. For a moment she'd forgotten Macon was there. "Do we still have onions?"

Macon stepped back from the trash bin. "Uh, we usually have a bag lying around. I know Javier went to the farmer's market this morning."

She stood up, her heart pounding. It was an onion. A stupid onion. She could beat an onion. "Good."

Jules turned and walked up the stairs and into the kitchen, her whole being focused on one task. One task that she was going to master. One perfect dice.

The kitchen was quiet but Javi, Sebastian, and Chef Taggart were talking quietly in the back. One of those men would have what she needed.

Tiffany walked through the double doors, menus in hand. She

stopped, obviously surprised to see her. "Hey, I thought you'd left."

"I need a knife." She didn't want to make small talk. She had to do this now or never.

Tiffany's eyes widened. "I...you...I don't know that a knife is the solution to your problems right now."

"Jules?" a familiar voice asked.

She turned and Javier was standing there. "I need a knife."

He didn't hesitate. He got his kit and rolled it out. "What type, sweetheart?"

"Are we sure about this? Sean, have you looked at her? You're the one who's always pointing out the crazy eyes," Macon said, walking in behind her.

"The chef's knife," Jules replied.

Sean shook his head Macon's way. "No. I'm not sure about anything except I'd like to see what happens next. Sometimes crazy is the only way things get done. Let her have it."

Javier passed her his beautifully kept chef's knife. The handle felt a little odd in her right hand. She was so used to it in her left that it sent a wave of melancholy through her. Fuck it. She would always miss her damn hand but she couldn't let it hold her back.

She'd learned it once. She could fucking learn it again. One door had closed and another had opened. She could choose to walk through the open one, to have another life. It would be an easy thing to do. Or she could bust that closed motherfucker down and take the life she'd always wanted.

"I need an onion." She turned, knowing without a doubt that Javier would provide one for her. He would find one here or he would go out and scour the damn city until he could bring one back to her. Because he was that kind of man. The kind she could count on. The kind she could build a life with if she only believed she was worthy.

There it was. The cutting board built for her because there was zero question in her mind that this hadn't been one of Javier's plans. He'd been trying to ease her into practicing, into taking back this part of her life. There was no one-armed chef coming in. There was only one of those at Top, and she had to prove herself. She had to do the work all over again. Start at the bottom and work her way up. And she would do it because this life was worth it. Because he was worth it.

"Here you go." Javier had a bag of plain white onions. There had to be thirty in there. They were likely meant for some ceviche or to flavor a sauce on the menu. It would be selfish to ruin them as she was likely to.

She took the first one because sometimes she had to be a little selfish.

"Let me show you, sweetheart," Javier said.

Chef stepped in. "No, she's not your sweetheart here and now. She's a chef and she's gotta learn." Sean Taggart stared at her, as intimidating as any master chief she'd ever had to face down. "I want a medium chop on that onion and you will not leave your station until I am satisfied with your performance. Am I clear?"

Fucking military men. What the hell would she do without them? He was giving her a shot. "Yes, sir."

"Proceed."

No one was going to baby her. No one was going to help. Not this time. Later they would be all about family and friends and pitching in, but this first time it had to be her. She had to stand on her own two feet and acknowledge that while her world had changed, she could hold fast to what mattered.

She could find herself. She could know who she was. She could choose who she wanted to be.

A badass bitch who wouldn't let a damn onion beat her.

This was what Javier had been doing. He hadn't learned it all to try to show her up or be better than she was. He'd learned it because he loved her and wanted to know what she went through. He'd tried to force her today because he'd known she would never be happy without this.

She used the prosthetic to stabilize the onion and started to cut it in half.

It flew out of her fake hand and tumbled to the floor.

Everyone was watching her. She would look like a fool.

Or she would look like a fighter.

Juliana leaned over and picked up the onion and began again.

Onion number three. Jules winced as she damn near sliced off her prosthetic thumb. She looked around at the wide-eyed crowd. "No blood. No foul. I'm fun to play with."

Onion number ten and the tears were rolling down her eyes. An hour and she'd barely managed a shit cut on the fuckers. She'd ruined ten of them, and everyone was still there. Still standing silent and watching. Her audience. She made the side cut and split this one, cracking it.

Onion number fourteen. Her hand was going numb. This was stupid. Her mother had offered to buy her a high-tech new hand and once she'd mastered that she might not even need the stupid cutting board. She groaned, her lower back aching as she made the mid cut. Not too thin. Not too thick. She had to get it right or the onion would fall apart when she started to chop it.

Onion number seventeen. Jules stepped back, presenting the veg to Chef.

Sean stared down. "Do you call that a medium chop? Would you want huge chunks of onion in your soup?"

She bit back a groan and tossed it all in the garbage.

Onion twenty-three.

Two o'clock in the morning and Ally was asleep on Macon's lap, her head resting against her husband's chest. Javier looked grim as he took the second to last onion out of the bag and passed it to her.

"You know Rome wasn't built in a day," he said.

"Chopping an onion isn't building a city," Sean shot back. "Do you think I want to be here at two in the morning? I do not. But I will stand here until she shows me a medium chop. She's not done."

She was. She wanted to cry because she was so fucking tired. Her eyes were dry from the fumes. There was nothing in the world she wanted more than to throw that damn onion in Chef's face and let Javier carry her home.

But she wasn't about to let Taggart beat her. No fucking way was she giving in. He thought he could stand there all night, well, she could show him.

Which, she believed, was exactly his point.

Press down. Hold. Center cut.

Press down. Traction. Begin midline cuts. Easy and slow because she wasn't good with this hand yet, but, oh, she could be. She felt it now. Even when her every muscle wanted to give in, she could feel the habits reforming. Time. Effort. Work.

All even cuts. As uniform as could be. She started from the outside now and worked her way in until it was done. Until she had a beautiful pile of onions, ready to be used in one of the finest restaurants in town.

She turned to her boss.

Chef looked down and picked through the pile, looking for pieces that were too big or too small. He finally nodded. "Juliana, you're fired."

"What?" Javier said, his shoulders straightening as he stood up.

But she knew what Chef was doing and her eyes weren't dry anymore. Everything hurt in the best way possible. "Yes, sir. When do I start my new job, sir?"

"Tomorrow. You'll do the prep work for me and Javier. I'll leave you with a list of what we'll need. When you're done prepping our dishes, you'll work on salads the rest of the night. We'll give it a few months and see where it goes." Sean put his hands on her shoulders. "And welcome to Top, Jules. You always belonged here. You simply needed to prove it to yourself."

Tiffany smiled as she popped open a bottle of champagne.

Ally sat straight up, her eyes flying open. "Did she kill the onion?"

Macon put an arm around his wife. "She killed it good, babe. Now we're having champagne."

"Ah, I woke up for the fun part," Ally said with a smile.

This was her new family and they'd stayed to support her, to celebrate with her. But she really only needed one more thing to make the night complete. A kiss from her man.

"I'm happy for you, Jules." Javier gave her a smile and started to step back. "You're going to be a great member of the team."

She frowned even as she was given her glass.

It looked like her fight wasn't over yet.

Chapter Ten

Javier walked alongside her, his whole soul sagging. He knew he should be elated. It had worked. She'd done it and she'd done it in spectacular fashion. This was exactly what he'd wanted for her all along.

But it was hard to be happy because she wouldn't be his. She would be in the kitchen now, closer than ever, and never more far away from him.

He opened the door to the building, allowing her to walk in first. "After you."

She walked past him, a tired smile on her face. "Thanks for giving me a ride."

"Of course."

It was past late. The lobby was completely silent and he could see Harold busy napping in the back. He needed to find a place with better security. He needed to find a new place, period, because living close to Jules and not being able to have her was going to be hell. She needed to focus on her career. She needed to be safe, and being around Rafe wasn't safe.

What the hell was he going to do about Rafe? Besides talk to him and ask him flat out what he was doing. If Rafe lied, he would go through his brother's things. It wasn't fair, but he had to know. If his brother was in trouble, he needed to find a way to get him out.

"So are we not going to talk anymore?" She settled her duffel bag over her shoulder. He'd asked if he could carry it for her, but she'd been stubborn. Sometime before they'd left she'd gone into the locker room and taken off her prosthetic, slipping it into a bag she kept in her locker for such an occasion.

"What do you mean? We've been talking the whole way home." They'd talked about the menus for the next week, what they would need, how she would adapt the board to be able to properly prep each veg. She'd talked about getting a new arm with a more technologically cutting-edge hand. Her mother was helping her pay for it.

How long would it be before her mother realized Jules could run her kitchens? How long before she snatched her daughter back?

"I meant are we going to talk about us?" Jules asked.

He sighed and started down the hall. "I thought we decided that earlier tonight, Jules. There's nothing left to talk about. I meant what I said. I'm not going to hurt you anymore. The truth is I'm not good at commitment."

He'd wondered if she would be on a high from the night and want to revisit that particular subject. It wasn't like he hadn't seen it before. Women sometimes came looking for him because they'd gotten a promotion or done something they'd only dreamed of, and they went to a club, high on the adrenaline and pride, and looked for someone to celebrate with. A little present to themselves. He hadn't minded then. It had been a fun game, and hey, if a lady wanted a prize, he could give her one.

It wasn't a game with Jules.

"You aren't good at commitment?" Jules asked.

This was what he'd come up with. He would give her the truth. It was what he should have done in the first place, but he hadn't been honest with himself, either. "I don't know if you've heard, but I have quite the reputation."

"Getting bored already?" There was a suspicious tone to her voice.

He stopped in front of the elevator. It would be the best way to cut the ties between them. He could look her straight in the eyes and tell her he wasn't getting what he needed sexually, that he couldn't imagine living the rest of his life with only one sex partner.

He couldn't do it. Not only was he a shitty liar, he couldn't look at her and willfully make her heart ache.

"Of course not." How to make her understand? "It's not about the sex. I think I've made it clear how much I enjoy making love to you. I'm not good at relationships. I haven't had many, and the ones I have been in didn't last for long. I wish it could be different, but it's not, and that's obvious to me."

And he'd fumbled with her. He'd pushed her when he shouldn't, stepped back when he should have taken control. He was a mess when it came to her.

"Awesome," she replied, pressing the button to go up. "I was worried it was something serious. I've got a solution for you, babe. Try harder. I think that was your advice to me and it worked perfectly." She breezed into the elevator and turned, leaning against the back wall and giving him a sultry smile. "I'm sure you'll work it out. Until then, try to think of our intimate time together as playing. If you need boundaries, we'll talk about it. We'll negotiate. That should get you through the rough first part."

He hopped on before the doors closed, knife set in his hand. It was rolled up and tied. He'd already thought about getting one for Jules. She needed a new one, one that was personally hers, used and taken care of by her. He didn't like the idea that she would have to use one of the restaurant's sets. She should have the best. Perhaps he could convince her Top always welcomed a new chef with a thousand dollars' worth of knives.

Yeah, she would buy that.

"What do you mean 'rough' part?" She wasn't making a ton of sense, but then they both needed sleep.

"The part where you pretend you never said you loved me, never spent days and days practicing to cook with one hand. The part where you decide to let me go for my own good, but we still end up in bed together because I intend to be naked around you as often as possible and you're not great with the self-control thing. That part."

Riding high was exactly what she was doing. She thought she'd conquered the world and now their problems had dissolved. But he knew they hadn't. "I don't think it's a good idea. I think you might be right about Rafe, and that makes him dangerous to be around."

"The good news is I'm pretty good at defending myself and I intend to take over for you there. He's your big brother. He's not mine. I'm going to explain the way of the world to him. He can go to rehab or he can go to jail."

"Jail?"

Her face softened. "I know it sounds harsh, but I'm not going to allow him to ruin your life. You're too close to this. I love you. I'll fight your brother for you."

Sweet words, but after the night she'd had, they were also inevitable. She'd climbed the highest of mountains, but tomorrow she would see they still had their problems. "I can't tell you how much that means, but I'll handle Rafe."

"Babe, unless you can admit that he has a real problem, you can't handle Rafe," she replied, moving into his space. She set the bag down and brought up her right hand to touch his face. "I'll find a good rehab center, and I know how to maneuver my way through the system. I'll make it work. And I'll do it for selfish reasons. I'm going to be honest. I don't want to live with your brother for the rest of my life. He's crabby, and I like a little peace at home."

The very touch of her hand sent a heat wave through his body. He had to step back because suddenly that elevator was too small for the two of them. "You don't have to live with Rafe. Honestly, I'm thinking about changing things up. I need to look for something a little bigger."

"We can get a house later," she said, her eyes on him. "I think for now it's best we stay close to the restaurant. Besides, I signed a year's lease. You might be out of yours, but I need to stay for another ten

176

months or so. Then we can talk."

"Jules, you're not listening to me."

"Javier, make some sense and I'll listen," she replied, backing him against the metal wall. She was so close she brushed against his cock.

"You can't say no to this." He cleared his throat because those words had come out all husky when he needed to be firm. "I broke up with you. That's not something you can say no to."

"Watch me. I fought tonight. I did that because you cared enough about me to push me. I am not going to give you up now." She put a hand on his chest as though challenging him to push her back. Or as though claiming him. She touched him like he belonged to her. Like they belonged together. "I know I hurt you earlier because I accused you of a bunch of stuff you didn't do, and now you think you need to throw yourself on your sword and spare me the heartache of loving you. But I'm strong. I can handle anything that comes my way, including dealing with whatever it is your brother is into. Including being your lowest employee at work."

"I don't mistreat my line chefs." If that was what she was worried about, she hadn't spent enough time in his kitchen.

"No, but you yell at them. You push them like hell because you want them to be better." She looked up at him, her eyes gleaming in the low light. "I can handle anything you dish out, Chef. I'll do my best and respect your authority. When we're working together, you're the boss. And when the lights go down and everyone else leaves, you can give me my daily performance review. Can you imagine how that will go?"

Yep. He had that vision in his head now. He'd thought he was tired, but there was a part of him that had come to vibrant, demanding life. "Jules…"

Her voice went low, the tone reminding him of how she moaned when he fucked her hard. "I imagine you'll punish me if I get something wrong. I probably will. Especially in the beginning. You'll keep a list of infractions and at the end of the day, I'll have to pay. I'll have to get undressed for you. You won't have it any other way and

177

I'll be a well-trained employee, so the minute the door locks and we're alone, you'll find me naked and kneeling, waiting for your notes."

She was killing him. His cock was already hard at the thought, and he could feel his blood starting to pound. "Juliana, this is serious."

"So were my infractions. This evening, I wasted an entire bag of onions. I think that likely deserves some punishment. Do you want to do it here?" Her face had brightened up, like a kitten eager to play.

"Playing" in this case meant burying his cock deep inside her.

He tried to push the idea out of his head. The one that contained his brain. The head on his dick had entirely different plans.

"The elevator doors will open any moment now." In fact, they'd been here for a while. It should not have taken them this long to get to the fourth floor. If he didn't get out of here soon, when those doors did open he would have her up against the wall, pounding himself inside her.

"Don't worry about it. I hit the *stop* button a long time ago," she whispered. "Ever done it in an elevator?"

A couple of times, but it would be different with her. Everything was different and new with her. "You're only saying these things because you had a breakthrough tonight. I don't want you to wake up tomorrow and regret this. And I would have gone out and bought another hundred onions if you'd needed them."

She put her hands on his chest. "I knew that. Do you know how I knew that? Because no one in my life has ever taken care of me the way you do. You say you're not good at commitment, but I'm going to have to argue with you. How many men would spend their free time practicing knife skills with a hand they would never use in the actual kitchen? How many hours did you spend on that? Learning what it would be like to be me in order to help me? That sounds like commitment to me. If it's not, I'll take it."

He'd done it so he could feel closer to her. She was a puzzle and he would never learn all her pieces, but he could spend a lifetime trying to put them all together, each forming a new and gorgeous section of the woman he was utterly fascinated with. He'd done it to know what she went through in a day because he'd never wanted to feel closer to a human being than he did this one.

He wanted to do everything she'd said. God, he wanted to play with her. He was tired beyond anything and he still wanted to get his hands on her. He could spank her and fuck her and sleep beside her.

Where? On his fucking sleeper sofa that he had to pull out to even get to?

In the same place that had been broken into twice in the last few weeks?

Meeting her mother had brought into crystal clarity exactly what he didn't have to offer her.

He reached out and touched the button to start the elevator again. "I think this is a mistake."

Jules frowned, but held up her hand in obvious submission. "If you need time, I'll give it to you, but don't try sliding back into your old habits. It won't go well for you or whoever you try to backslide with. Can we agree on that?"

His old habits? He knew what she meant. He worried he might never have those old habits again.

"I don't want anyone but you," he said quietly. She might have ruined him for all other women, and wasn't that the funniest fucking part? "I don't even think about other women. But I don't think I'm good for you."

She stared forward. "You're wrong. And I'm going to prove it to you. You, Javier Leones, are the absolute best thing that ever happened to me."

The doors opened and he couldn't help but reach for her hand. He brushed against it and then thought better, but her fingers were already tangled with his. They meshed easily, as if that was their natural state.

He couldn't work up the will to let her go. He would walk her to her apartment. He would not go in. He would not follow her inside and ease her clothes off and make long, slow love to her until they both fell into an exhausted sleep.

They walked down the hall in silence.

As they started to pass his apartment, the door came open and a man dressed all in black stepped out into the hallway. All in black except for the silver gun in his hand.

"Mr. Leones, I thought you were going to disappoint us this evening. Please, come inside. We've been trying to make a deal with your brother, but he's unable to satisfy us. I hope you can do better."

Fear flooded his system. Not for himself. For her. He dropped her hand and tried to look like a dude who dealt with drug dealers all the time. There was no question in his mind that the man in front of him was just that. Or some kind of mobster, but he thought the former because the man was dressed in sweats and a T-shirt, a bandana around his neck that likely symbolized what gang he worked for.

"Go on, babe. I'll take care of this and be down there in a bit." He winked her way like it was no big deal.

Jules sighed. "I told you he was using. He didn't even bother to offer us any. Your brother's an asshole."

She was good. There was nothing at all in her manner that suggested fear or that this was anything but an ordinary, everyday occurrence.

But when she started to step away, the man moved in front of her. Javier reached out, pulling her back.

"I don't think so," the man said. "I think you both should come inside." He glanced down at her. "Looks like you already had some trouble, honey. Be a good girl or you'll lose the other hand."

Rage rose, a cobra needing to strike.

"Men," Jules said with a sigh. "You're always so dramatic."

She squeezed his hand as though to remind him that his rage wouldn't stop a bullet.

He took a deep breath, tamping down his emotions. "Still think I'm the best thing that ever happened to you?"

She rolled her eyes and strode into his apartment.

He had to pray he found a way to stop whatever was about to happen because he couldn't lose her.

He couldn't.

* * * *

Jules followed the asshat drug lord into Javier's apartment and managed to not tell her reluctant boyfriend that she told him so. Well, she kind of had before, but she'd used it as cover in an attempt to get the asshat to let her go to her own apartment. Once there, she would have contacted the police, gotten her gun, and shown back up to save her reluctant boyfriend because he couldn't transform into her eager boyfriend if he was dead.

But when they were through with this, he was getting an *I told you so*. A hearty one.

She stopped as she took in the scene before her. Or maybe she would just wrap her arms around him and hold him tight.

His brother was on the floor, his wheelchair busted, and it looked like someone had broken it over Rafael's body. He had his shirt off, a pair of cutoff sweat pants the only clothing he had on. He looked so vulnerable without his chair or prosthetics.

Her heart constricted as Javier tried to go to his brother. Was he even alive? There was a lot of blood, and she couldn't see his left eye anymore. It was swollen shut. There was a bloody gag in his mouth.

How long had he been here, being beaten and tortured? They had music playing through the room. Not anything so loud that the neighbors would call the police, but loud enough it might cover the sounds of fists hitting flesh.

"What the hell did you do to him?" Javier asked, kneeling beside his brother. He set his knife kit on the chair beside the couch.

Jules watched, waiting to see if they would take it. She set down her bag and gingerly moved to where she could stand in front of the chair. They might not realize what it was. To the layman it would look like a small, cylindrical leather bag.

Javier pulled the gag out of his brother's mouth and tossed it to the side.

"Nothing I didn't promise I would do weeks ago," the asshat said with a long sigh. "Isn't that right, Rafe? This has been a long time coming. You thought you could move and I wouldn't figure out where you were, did you?"

"Mac, if you hurt Sonja," Rafe started, his voice ragged

Mac held up his free hand. "I'm a gentleman. And your wife is actually respectable. I don't play around with innocent women and kids. That's a good way to go to jail. Besides, she's smart, too. She kicked you out. She's not going to help pay your bill, is she? She'd let you die, but I bet your brother here won't say the same thing."

They weren't alone. Another man strode out of the bedroom, a gun in his hand as well. He was shorter, skinny enough that she would bet he sampled the product, and often. "I can't find it, Mac. He says it's somewhere in there, but I don't see it."

"I bet his brother knows, Greg." Mac knelt down beside Javier. "Let's talk, you and I. Now I'm a reasonable man. I understand fully that you owe me nothing. It's your addict brother who's run up a considerable bill that apparently he can't pay. My product isn't free. I offered your brother credit because I felt for him. I love our troops, too, man."

Rafe turned his face up, a moan coming from his mouth. "I'm sorry, Javi. I tried to get the money. I really did."

God, she wished she hadn't been right. "How much does he owe?"

Javier stood up, putting his body in front of hers. "Leave her out of this. He's my brother and I'll take care of whatever I need to."

"Your brother here tells me you have a safe and that's where you keep the serious cash," Mac said, his voice low.

"I don't have serious cash," Javier argued, his face pained. "I have about twenty-five hundred dollars in cash. I can get another grand from the bank. That's all."

Mac followed him. "Well, that is a problem because your brother owes ten grand."

"You took ten thousand dollars' worth of pills?" Javier asked, horror plain in his voice.

Mac shrugged. "There might be some penalties and interest involved in that particular number, but that's the only number my boss is going to accept."

"I don't have that kind of cash," Javier replied.

Mac did not look like a man who was ready to negotiate. "But I bet you could get it. I bet there's a lot of money running through that restaurant you work at."

Jules kept quiet, watching the second man. He seemed much more interested in Javier than in her. Likely they looked at her arm and thought she was perfectly harmless. She was cool with that, but she hadn't been in the Navy for her health. She hadn't slept through training either. She'd enjoyed the physical aspects of the military.

She eased the case onto her lap while they were arguing.

"No one pays cash at restaurants these days," Javier was saying. "Top isn't some fast-food place. Everyone pays with credit these days. I don't know how my working there is going to help you. Though maybe you should come in one night. My boss might help me out. He might be able to float me some cash. Just give me until tomorrow night, man. I can get it for you. Meet me at the backdoor of the kitchen and we'll make the exchange then."

And ten former military men would be waiting for Mac. Most of them Special Forces. It was a brilliant plan. They'd bring Big Tag in for fun. She heard the dude liked some violence from time to time.

Her man was smart.

Mac frowned down at him. "I promised I would have the money tonight. I have obligations, too."

Javier held his hands up. "All right. I'll call him now. He can meet us."

She gently twisted the strap on the left side of the knife kit.

Sean Taggart would be pissed to have his sleep interrupted, but he would also take care of the situation. Likely in a super-bloody way. She kind of hoped she got to see that, but she had to plan for the worst-case scenario.

"You really think this friend can come through for you?" Mac asked.

Javier nodded. "He's got the money. He can get it in cash, but we'll have to meet him."

She had her hand on the second buckle. Maybe she wouldn't have to do this after all. If the Taggarts were about to get involved, she would happily sit in the audience and watch. She wasn't a fool. She would leave it to the experts. And then her man would get a reward for thinking so fast on his feet. After they'd carted his brother off to a very nice rehab facility.

"What about Mom's ring?" Rafe croaked out the words. "I know she gave it to you to keep in the safe. It's worth a lot."

Or screw rehab. She could kill him.

"Let's see it." Mac waved the gun Javier's way. "Where's the safe? I want the cash and I want to see that ring. I don't like the idea of taking this show on the road."

Yep, she was going to kill Rafe.

"What the fuck is that?" Mac asked, turning to her.

She picked the knife kit up, holding it close and trying to look super scared. "It's my art work. I'm working with a small canvas right now. I roll it up so I can take it with me. Do you want to see it?"

He frowned. "Do I want to see your fucking art work? Is it worth ten grand?"

She shook her head. "No. I've never actually sold anything, but I'm trying."

"With one fucking hand," he said with a roll of his eyes. "Just shut the fuck up while your boyfriend here gets me what I need. If he doesn't, well, I might have to take you with me to make sure he behaves."

Javier's eyes were wide as he looked back at her. "Just be calm, Jules. I'll handle this. Let me handle this."

He was pleading with her because he knew what was in that pack, but she couldn't let the chance go by. Maybe if Javier gave them enough they would let all three of them live, but why risk it? They'd said each other's names, allowed them to see their faces. It wasn't looking good.

"Where's the safe? I'm getting impatient," Mac said. "Greg, watch these two. Make sure the cripples don't get away."

She clutched her kit like she was going to cry.

Javier led Mac back into his bedroom.

There wasn't a lot she could do with that Greg person looking right at her.

"So you're some kind of artist, huh? Don't let Mac get to you," he said, moving into her space. "I think you're pretty even with the bum arm. If you have to come with us, stay close to me. I'll take care of you."

"You going to take care of her with that tiny dick of yours?" Rafe rasped out.

Greg's head swung around to look at Rafe. "What the fuck did you say?"

Rafe's lips curved up in a bloody grin. "I heard some of the women at that club your boss runs talking about what a tiny little needle dick you have."

She gasped as Greg's booted foot came out and then met Rafe's gut with a horrific thud.

"You want to say that again, asshole?" Greg asked, his attention focused wholly on his victim.

Thereby giving her the time she needed to get that sucker open. Rafe knew what she was holding, too. He was trying to cover for her. Rafe said something truly terrible to the man and Greg went at him again.

She got the kit opened, unrolling it quickly. Javier had two boning knives, one for fish and poultry, a second with a stiffer blade for pork and beef. Six inches long, it would be far easier to handle than the chef knife.

She shoved the kit back onto the table and thanked the universe for men who thought anything with breasts was harmless and something to turn one's back on. And she silently thanked Rafe for taking one for the team. Hard.

Greg kicked him in the gut.

Jules took that moment to stab him in the right arm, the powerful knife slicing through muscle and sinew exactly as it was supposed to.

And her opponent did what came naturally when one's arm was being assaulted. His hand lost its grip, dropping the gun as he shouted out.

Jules started to go for the weapon, but Rafe had it in his hands, and he proved he hadn't spent all that time in the military for nothing either.

Rafe rolled and raised his hand and took the shot.

Greg stumbled back, his hand on his chest, trying to stop the blood.

Mac showed up in the doorway, pointing his gun toward Jules first.

It didn't matter. Javier was on his back, his arm going around Mac's neck in a choke hold.

Rafe reached out and dragged Jules to the floor, trying to cover her with his body. "Stay down. Let Javier take care of him. He's good at this. I should know. The little shit perfected it on me when we used to wrestle."

She needed to get up, to help Javi. The problem was while Rafe might not like to use what was left of his legs, he had some serious upper-body strength.

There was a thud and then Javier was standing over her, his face pale. He reached out, hauling her up.

"I thought I told you to let me handle it," he said, dragging her close.

"You also told me I was good with knives." She was shaking, the adrenaline still coursing through her.

The door came open and all heads turned.

Mrs. Gleeson stood there in her gown, a shotgun in her hand. She looked around the room. "Did you leave any for me?"

"Damn it, old woman." Mr. Cassidy ran in, adjusting his glasses. There was a cell phone in his hand. "I told you to wait for the police."

Javier sighed and squeezed her tight as they heard the sirens.

She held on, promising herself she would never let go again.

Chapter Eleven

"**Y**ou sure you want to close up?" Sean Taggart crossed his arms over his chest and frowned Javier's way. "You had a long day. I don't mind finishing up here."

Long day? It had been a heinous day. First there had been the police to deal with. Then he'd had to deal with Rafael. That was even worse than the police because he'd had to deal with Rafe on his own. While he'd dealt with the police and watched his brother's drug dealers get hauled off, he'd had Jules at his side. When they'd left and he'd been forced to confront his brother, he'd asked her to leave.

He was fairly certain that had hurt her. Something he'd promised never to do again, but then he was also the man who'd promised not to put her in danger and he'd forced her to stab a criminal.

"It's your date night with Grace," he replied. "I can handle it by myself. I'll reconcile the books and lock up."

Sean put a hand on his shoulder. "I appreciate it. And I wouldn't call it a date night so much as a play night. We're going to spend some time in the pool house. I can't make it to Sanctum this weekend. Our little space will have to do. Grace's mom has the kids for the night. With two young kids, we don't get to play much. That's my advice to you. Play as much as you can before the babies start coming."

"I don't think that's happening any time soon." Jules had barely spoken to him all night. She'd texted him in the afternoon, explaining she was going in early, and then she'd been polite all evening long. Jules had done exactly what she should have done—concentrated on her job. It was what he needed to do now.

Now that Rafe was in rehab. He'd managed to get his brother to commit to a 21-day program. From there they would have to see.

He'd called Sonja and she'd even promised to come in for family therapy.

"These things happen when you least expect them, my friend. Hey, how did the new girl do?"

Javier forced himself to smile. "She was great."

Sean shook his head slightly. "I don't know. She wasted a couple of bell peppers and the chop on those potatoes had to be redone twice. It was a good thing she came in early. She's going to have to practice hours a day."

"She's trying. She'll be amazing one day. You'll see." He wasn't sure he liked how negative Sean was being.

"I'm just saying, she's your employee. She's yours to deal with, and I don't think you should go easy on her. I think she wants something entirely different," Sean said enigmatically. "The books are in my office. Make sure you clean up when you're done. I'm serious about that. You'll be the one in trouble if that office isn't pristine. And use the anti bac. Everyone freaking knows where it is."

Why would he need anti bac to enter the daily numbers into the system and check inventory?

He didn't ask. Chef could be weird and as sarcastic as his older brother when he wanted to be.

Eventually he was sure Jules would want to talk to him, but it looked like she'd given up for the time being. And that was a good thing. At least that's what he told himself.

She'd cleaned up her station and then he hadn't seen her after that.

How had she gotten home? He hadn't seen her car. Had she taken the train and walked two blocks by herself? Hopefully one of the guys who took the train had been with her for that part. He knew she could take care of herself, but bad shit happened and he couldn't stand to think about it happening to her.

He closed the blinds and turned off the inner lights. He would go out the back way where his truck was parked.

He couldn't help but look at the spot where he'd danced with Jules the day before. He'd held her and said good-bye because he couldn't do anything else.

The only woman he would ever love.

He'd made the right choice. They both needed to focus on work. He had to help his brother. He was certain the last thing Jules needed was more sad-sack therapy sessions, and that's what she would get because if he'd stayed with her, he would be in deep and he wouldn't have pretended. Jules would be his family and he would want her with him always. He would want to talk to her and have her help him figure out what to do. Meet his mother and his little niece.

It didn't matter what he wanted because he fully intended to back her play from today.

When she finally came to him and said she thought they should talk, he would sit down with her and graciously let her go.

And if she was still here when his family got their shit sorted out, he would go after her like she'd never been gone after before. If she wasn't smart enough to get away from him, he would catch her and hold her and never let her go. A year. Maybe in a year he could get everything together so he would have something real to give her. A home. A family that wasn't fucked up beyond all recognition. A life he would be proud to share with her.

He moved back to Chef's office and opened the door, ready to spend an hour on the boring shit, but this was what it took to run a restaurant. One day he would have his own and he would know the boring crap because Sean Taggart made him learn it.

He opened the door and stopped in his tracks because he wasn't alone.

Juliana was sitting on the leather couch, a towel under her. She needed the towel because she was completely and utterly naked. She sat there with her red hair spilling over her shoulders. It curled around her breasts, nipples peeking through. Her long legs were crossed so he couldn't see her pussy, but he knew how lovely it was, knew he would see it soon.

Because fuck waiting. She was here. She was naked and offering herself to him, and all the reasons he wasn't going to do this were gone, and not because of his dick. His dick could wait.

His heart…that was another impatient bastard altogether.

"I know you think we should wait," she began.

He was walking toward her and she stood suddenly, her eyes wide and startled, as though she wasn't sure what he would do next. Did she think he would throw her out? Think he would impose his will on her?

He needed her too fucking much.

He strode to her, not stopping until he wrapped his arms around her and pulled her in close. He breathed in her unique scent. This was what he'd needed for hours and hours. For days. For his entire fucking life.

Jules's hugged him tight and she rubbed her cheek against his. "I thought you might be mad."

"I'm not, but I am weak. I know this is not a good time, but, baby, I'm not going to be able to let you go."

"You shouldn't. This is the perfect time, Javi. You need me and there's absolutely nowhere in the world I would rather be. I hated the fact that you sent me home this morning. My home is at your side. Nowhere else."

His parents hadn't hesitated to lean on each other. He was letting what happened to his brother's marriage affect his relationship with Juliana, but that wasn't the marriage he should look to. His parents had been steadfast and loving through many bad times. They hadn't tried to shove the other away. They had clung to each other, halving the burdens, doubling the joys of life.

"I love you," he whispered. "I'm not ever letting you go again. I promise."

"If you do, I'll come after you."

And he knew how good she was getting with knives. "I'll remember that."

He kissed her forehead and stepped back.

She'd promised him something else. She'd promised him after-hours play, and now he understood what Sean had meant by playing as much as they could before those pesky, amazing babies started coming. Babies who would have their mother's spirit. Babies who would make everything difficult and awesome and worthwhile.

But for now, they could play.

"How many peppers did you waste tonight?"

Her eyes flared and then dropped in submission. He watched as her whole body relaxed, knowing it was going to get something so fucking good. "Far too many, Chef, but please remember I'm learning."

He walked slowly around her, inspecting that gorgeous body of hers. She'd ditched her prosthetic. He loved that she was comfortable around him without it. She should be. There wasn't an inch of her that wasn't pure perfection to him. Every scar was proof of her strength, and he loved them all. "Yes, and part of your learning must be discipline. I thought I was clear about that."

She looked up, her eyes alight with mischief. "I thought this part was totally my idea."

Brat. "How quickly you forget. I believe I introduced you to role-play, sweetheart."

"But I'm perfecting it. When you think about it, it's kind of like our relationship in the kitchen. You come up with a decent idea for a dish and I make it better."

So very arrogant, and it was good to see. A chef had to have some arrogance in her. One day, they would work side by side. She would catch up and possibly surpass him, and it would be a glorious fight that would always end in the bedroom or the dining room or the broom closet. Wherever it was easiest to get inside her.

"I think we're going to have to talk about how quick you are to criticize my dishes." He let his voice go low. "One thing I'm going to insist on from you is respect."

Her mouth formed a perfect *O*. "Babe, I was joking."

"And I'm playing, which proved I'm so much better at it than you."

She relaxed and he saw her smile before she let her eyes find the floor again. "Yes, Chef. I truly do respect you. I hope you'll allow me to show you how much I respect you."

He could think of a few ways she could show him. "I believe you owe me at least twenty." Not a lot. Just barely enough to get her ass warm. She was still a playful tourist. One day she would be able to take fifty and beg him for more. "Place your elbows on the desk and show me that perfect ass."

She moved to the desk, lowering herself down and presenting her ass to him. "Like this, Chef?"

He put a hand on her, loving the thrum of connection he felt the minute he touched her. His body came alive when she walked in a room, but he swore he could feel his blood begin to pound when he touched her. He let his hands skim her skin, running over her backside. "Yes, this will do. Spread your legs wider."

She took a deep breath and eased her legs open until he could step between them. "Better?"

He had access to her pussy. That made everything better. "Yes. You don't have to stay silent. No one's here. If you feel the need to cry out, do so. It won't bother me at all."

"Sadist," she said under her breath.

Oh, tomorrow she was getting some nipple clamps. He brought his hand back and smacked her backside hard.

He was rewarded with a squeal and some pretty squirming.

"You should be happy I'm in such a good mood," he said as he spanked her again. And again. And again.

Her lovely skin was a rosy pink after ten.

Her chest shuddered as she dragged in a breath. Her face rested on one side and he could see she was biting her bottom lip. She whimpered and her breath fluttered out. He would bet her nipples would be hard and wanting.

"Where are you?" He wanted to be sure. They'd played so little that he couldn't know one hundred percent that she was with him. After they'd had a hundred sessions, he would be able to read her every move, every breath to tell if she was close to the edge or needed something different entirely.

And he'd likely still want to hear the words from her mouth.

"I'm dying. It hurts and it's not enough. It's slow torture because I can't wait to get to what comes next. I've wanted this all night. It was difficult to keep my mind on my work because I knew we would be here in a few hours."

She'd thought about this all night? He'd been morose and she'd been waiting in anticipation. His hand came down. Five quick smacks. "Next time, mention it to your Master that you intend to rock his world."

"I thought that might send you running," she admitted on a cry.

"I have zero self-control when it comes to you. I think I would have done exactly what I did when I walked into this room." Of course, then he would have had a horrible hard-on all night, so maybe he owed her. Not that he would tell her that.

"I'll remember that next time," she vowed over the sound of his hand smacking her ass. "Next time, I'll make sure you know exactly what's waiting for you at the end of a long, hard day."

Long and hard described him perfectly, and it was time to do something about that.

He wrapped an arm around her waist and helped her stand, letting his erection rub against the ass he'd just warmed up beautifully.

She leaned back into him, allowing him to run his hands up her body to cup her breasts. There were those perky nipples and yes, they were hard against his palms. That ass he'd smacked rubbed and cuddled up against his hard-on, getting him even harder.

"I'm sure you're going to make things very difficult for me in the kitchen occasionally, but you should know that I'll be more than happy to take it out on your pretty ass every single time," he promised. "Now I need to know something. How did you like that spanking? Do you think it's going to help you to be better tomorrow?"

"I don't know, Chef," she admitted, her voice husky. "I think I need more."

He needed so much more. He couldn't stop until he'd had it all. Everything she had to give him. "I don't know if you're ready for more. I'm going to need you to prove it to me. How can I know the spanking did what it was supposed to do if you don't show me?"

He released her and stepped back, giving her plenty of space.

She turned. "I assure you, Chef. I'm one dish that is perfectly ready to be served."

"How can I know until you give me a little taste?"

"Well, I don't have a spoon for you," she said. "But I've been reminded lately that adaptation can be good for the soul."

She ran her hand down her body, letting her palm run between her breasts and down her belly, and lower. One single finger ran across her glistening clitoris and between her labia. When she brought it up, that finger was coated in her own arousal. She crossed the space between them and offered it up to her Master. "I think you'll find this to your liking, Chef."

Oh, he found everything about her to his liking. There was nothing he would change. He gripped her wrist gently and brought her hand to his lips. He sucked her finger into his mouth, her unique flavor coating his tongue. He made sure he didn't leave a single drop behind.

"Yes, I think that's perfectly prepared, but you know sometimes you have to let a dish rest for a few minutes," he said because he wasn't ready to dive in yet. He wanted to make it last. "I think I need you to make sure I'm ready, too."

"You aren't ready at all, Chef." Her hands went to his T-shirt. He'd shed his jacket before cleanup. "Should I help you?"

"Undress me and let's see how ready I am for you." He could go right now, but it was better to make the moment last. No more quickies for him. He did the long, slow, all-night thing now. Sometimes they could start here in the restaurant and he would do it all over again when they got home.

She pulled the shirt over his head, showing she didn't need hands to get him undressed. He didn't even think about helping her because she was relishing doing it all herself. She used her good hand to flick open the buckle of his belt.

He should have known she could do that easily since she'd managed to get his knife kit open in the brief period of time he'd left her alone. "Jules, I swear you nearly killed me yesterday. Next time drugs dealers come after us, you have to let me handle it, sweetheart. My heart won't stand another episode like that one."

She dropped down to her knees. "But I was good. I think if I didn't like cooking so much, I might talk to Big Tag about working at McKay-Taggart. I would make a good spy."

He shook his head. "You're staying right here where I can watch you. Speaking of, I think I should move into your place. It's nicer than mine and we weren't almost murdered there."

"Yes, Chef," she agreed as she started to pull his slacks down. When she ran into a little trouble, she simply took one side between her teeth and eased them down.

His dick sprang free, desperate for her attention.

He managed to toe out of his loafers, and she swept the rest of his clothes away, leaving him perfectly naked with her. As he should be.

Jules sat back on her heels, obviously pleased with herself. Yeah, the fact that he could put that look on her face filled him with pride. She could hold herself apart, but there was nothing between them now, nothing at all that could keep them away from each other.

She smiled up at him, her eyes warm and welcoming. Her hand came up and she gripped his cock, proving she was definitely getting good at adapting. There was strength and skill in her grip.

"Put your mouth on me," he demanded, his hands finding her hair. She had to wear it up in the kitchen, neatly pinned and tucked in, but here she let it flow, the red glossy locks going everywhere. He fisted his hands in her hair and tugged lightly.

She moved in, kissing the head of his cock first before slowly letting her lips close around him. He felt the first lick of her tongue and had to steady himself. He directed her movements, leading her with a slight pull here or a tug there. She followed his every wordless instruction, taking more and more of his cock with each pass.

He let her play, her tongue rolling over and around his cock. She hummed, the sound making his skin vibrate in a way he could feel in his balls.

After the longest time, he knew he couldn't wait another second and pulled back. He reached down and picked her up, bringing her to her feet and beyond so she was completely in his arms, her mouth close to his.

"I love it when you manhandle me," she said, lightly kissing his mouth. "You make me feel delicate."

She was—to him. He kissed her, letting their tongues play.

He backed her up to the desk and set her down there. Someone had prepped the space like the very good prep cook she was. There was a condom sitting right there, as though she knew all his moves and figured out where he would put her.

He ripped the package open and eased the condom on, watching her as she spread herself wide on the desk, welcoming him home.

"I'm going to marry you," he said, stepping between her legs and surrounding himself with her warmth.

"You bet you are," she replied, gasping as he thrust inside.

That was exactly how he liked her. Sassy. Bold. Taking what was hers, and he was so very hers.

Javier took what was his, too. That gorgeous body, that perfectly aligned soul. She moved her hips against his and he was off the leash.

He fucked her hard, every single thrust bringing them closer and closer to the edge. He twisted his hips, angling up and hitting that spot deep inside her that made her mouth come open, her eyes go wide as she sank her nails into his back and fought for her orgasm.

When it hit him, he held on, not wanting the moment to fade. He thrust in and pulled out, slamming back again and again until he was perfectly spent.

She lay back, her face flush, her lips in a brilliant smile. "Well, Chef, I think I will absolutely learn my lesson. I want to screw up a lot if that's my punishment."

The play was over and it was time for some truth. He leaned over and kissed her. "Have I told you how proud I am of you? Because I am."

"Have I told you how much I love you?" Jules asked. "Because I do."

He was just about to start all over again when the door flew open.

Javier covered Jules, but then relaxed slightly when he saw who it was. "Occupied, you two. You know damn well this is a sex space for employees only."

Big Tag and Charlotte stood in the doorway. His arm was still in a sling from the play party incident, but here the big guy was, still trying to get some. There was no question about that because his wife was only wearing a bra and barely there undies.

"Damn it," Tag cursed.

"I told you someone was here," Charlotte said, blushing but not backing down. If she minded looking at naked people who were literally still connected to each other, she didn't show it.

He needed to get them out of here and fast. "There's a very nice broom closet and it's got condoms and lube stashed behind the paper towels."

Big Tag nodded. "That'll do."

He dragged his wife off.

Jules's brows were high over her eyes. "Condoms and lube in the closet?"

He gave her a grin. "It's all for you, baby. Well, from now on."

Her arms came back up around his neck. "Forever."

Yes, he liked the way she thought.

Author's Note

I'm often asked by generous readers how they can help get the word out about a book they enjoyed. There are so many ways to help an author you like. Leave a review. If your e-reader allows you to lend a book to a friend, please share it. Go to Goodreads and connect with others. Recommend the books you love because stories are meant to be shared. Thank you so much for reading this book and for supporting all the authors you love!

Sign up for Lexi Blake's newsletter
and be entered to win a $25 gift certificate
to the bookseller of your choice.

Join us for news, fun, and exclusive content
including free short stories.

There's a new contest every month!

Go to www.LexiBlake.net to subscribe.

Master Bits & Mercenary Bites~Girls Night
Short Stories & Slices of Life by Lexi Blake
Recipes from Suzanne M. Johnson
Now available.

From the creators of *Master Bits and Mercenary Bites*, *New York Times* bestselling author Lexi Blake and Southern food expert and *USA Today* bestselling author Suzanne Johnson, comes a new look at the Masters and Mercenaries world—*Girls Night*.

Join us for easy to cook, delicious recipes and stay for the stories of the women of McKay-Taggart. From slow cooker special dinners to cocktails that will elevate your game, Suzanne will show you that easy can be delicious.

Lexi dives into what happens after happily ever after. Charlie and Ian try to have a night out—but their kids prove that anything can happen when Taggarts are involved. Faith and Ten get a gift they never expected. Karina and Derek go on a stakeout. And Serena finds the meaning of Bliss. All these stories and more explore what it means to be a wife, a mother, a woman navigating love and responsibility.

Good meals, good times, good friends.

Bon appétit!

* * * *

Excerpt from *Rough Night*

"You taste better than any pie, my Charlie," Ian whispered against her lips. His hands tightened on her and she felt one of those big palms stroke her thigh. "Why don't you straddle me and let's see what happens."

She knew what would happen. She placed the tray of treats on the table beside them and gingerly shifted, twisting so she straddled her Master's lap. Yes, there it was. His cock was right against her pussy. All she had to do was…

Ian groaned as she rolled her pelvis. "That's right, baby. Now give me some of that sweet, sweet lemony goodness. Ride me and feed me. That's what I want. Let me watch you come."

"And if I can make you come?" It was a fun little game. She would try to see if she could get that big dick of his to go off before she did.

"Then I'll walk around for the rest of the night a bit on the uncomfortable side," he replied, his hands finding her hips. He shifted and she found herself with her clitoris in the perfect position. "But that's not going to happen. I know exactly how to make you moan, Charlie baby."

She felt her phone vibrate. Charlie winced. "It's another text."

He pumped his hips up against hers. "Answer it. If it's anyone except Malone telling us one of the children is missing, I'm texting them a dick pic and asking them to leave us alone. Let's see if you can text while I do this."

His erection slid over the perfect place and Charlie could feel the orgasm starting to build. How could he still do this to her? All he had to do was start touching her, using that deep Dom voice on her, and her whole body was ready to comply to his any and every whim.

Did she have to answer? It probably wasn't anything important. Was anything in the world as important as the way this man made her feel?

"Give me a taste of that tart, baby. Or better yet, pull those pretty nipples out and let me taste them. Let me lick and suck and bite on those sweet nipples."

Her vision was going soft as he hauled her close.

And her phone vibrated again.

"Ian," she started.

"Do what you need to," he replied as he licked her collarbone. "I'll do what I have to."

She was going to kill whoever was texting her. It was probably Malone, trying to figure out where the damn marshmallows were.

She bit back a groan and reached for her phone. It better be so good because she was getting close, and the minute Ian started sucking on her breasts she wouldn't be able to hold…

Do you have a fire extinguisher?

"What?" Charlie shifted, trying to get a better grip on the phone.

And the chair under Ian kind of exploded.

Charlie hit the floor, her knees knocking on the tile. Ian had gone backward but he'd managed to twist his body so he landed on his shoulder instead of knocking the back of his head against the windowsill.

Panic flooded Charlie's veins. She scrambled to find her phone. "Ian?"

"I'm fine," he groaned. "Call him. Damn it. Can't we have one fucking night out without the world coming to an end? Ah, yeah, this is going to hurt."

Had he thrown out his back again? She couldn't stop and find out. Sarah Stevens was here somewhere and she was a nurse. Surely she could help.

Charlie grabbed the phone from the midst of the now fallen lemon tarts. The tray had turned over, but there were still several that had landed on the table. She would have to shove those in her purse if they were about to flee home. With shaking fingers she dialed the number for Michael.

"Hey, Charlotte, I think I got the fire out. Boomer stopped, dropped, and rolled on it. That did the trick. The girls thought it was hilarious, but we've got another problem now," Michael was saying.

"There was a fire?" She practically screamed the question.

"Tell Boomer to sit on it," Ian said from the floor. "Put him on speaker."

She didn't need his sarcasm, but he had the right to listen in. She clicked to go to speaker. "Where was the fire, Michael?"

"Well, you see when I told the girls we could have a campout in the living room, I kind of thought we would build a fort made out of sheets, you know what I'm talking about," Michael continued, his Texas drawl slow and steady. "Damn, Charlotte. I didn't think the girls would take it so literally."

Her girls took everything literally. "The girls tried to start a fire? In my living room?"

"It was minor," Michael promised. "Mostly because they couldn't take apart the furniture to burn. That was their plan. Apparently Ian taught them how to use whatever's around to stay warm in case they find themselves out in the woods at night. I saved the sofa, but they did manage to get that wicker basket of yours to burn. Kala said she had to use it because she couldn't get to the hatchet."

Charlie turned to her husband. "Why would our daughters know how to use a hatchet?"

He was a nice shade of pale and his shoulder seemed weird. "You told me to teach them some life skills."

She was going to kill everyone.

Nobody Does It Better
Masters and Mercenaries 15
By Lexi Blake
Now available.

A spy who specializes in seduction

Kayla Summers was an elite CIA double agent, working inside China's deadly MSS. Now, she works for McKay-Taggart London, but the Agency isn't quite done with her. Spy master Ezra Fain needs her help on a mission that would send her into Hollywood's glamorous and dangerous party scene. Intrigued by the mission and the movie star hunk she will be shadowing, she eagerly agrees. When she finds herself in his bed, she realizes she's not only risking her life, but her heart.

A leading man who doesn't do romance

Joshua Hunt is a legend of the silver screen. As Hollywood's highest paid actor, he's the man everyone wants to be, or be with, but something is missing. After being betrayed more than once, the only romance Josh believes in anymore is on the pages of his scripts. He keeps his relationships transactional, and that's how he likes it, until he meets his new bodyguard. She was supposed to keep him safe, and satisfied when necessary, but now he's realizing he may never be able to get enough of her.

An ending neither could have expected

Protecting Joshua started off as a mission, until it suddenly felt like her calling. When the true reason the CIA wanted her for this assignment is revealed, Kayla will have to choose between serving her country or saving the love of her life.

Chasing Taz
Charon MC, Book 3
By Khloe Wren
Now available.

The dramatic conclusion to the Charon MC Trilogy is here…

He lived his life one conquest at a time. She calculated her every move… until she met him.

Former Marine Donovan 'Taz' Lee might appear to be a carefree Aussie bloke living it up as a member of the Texan motorcycle club, Charon MC, but the truth is so much more complicated. With blood and tears haunting his past and threatening to destroy his future, Taz is completely unprepared for the woman of his dreams, when she comes in and knocks him on his ass. Literally.

Felicity "Flick" Vaughn joined the FBI to get answers behind her brother's dishonorable discharge and abandonment of his family. Knowing Taz was a part of her brother's final mission, she agrees to partner with him to go after a bigger club, The Satan's Cowboys MC.

However, nothing in life is ever simple and Flick is totally unprepared to have genuine feelings for the sexy Aussie. When secrets are revealed and their worlds are busted wide open, will they be strong enough to still be standing when the dust settles?

Other books in the series:
Inking Eagle, Book 1
Fighting Mac, Book 2
Go to http://www.khloewren.com/ for more information.

Excerpt:

Taz
Once Viper took possession of the ledger, he stood and led us out of the meeting room. I still had the digital copy we'd made back when we first found the books, so if any of the Cowboys went back on the

agreement, the feds would be getting a present. But no one needed to know about that.

"Let's go get your girl. I'll warn you, Stone doesn't want her going with you."

"He can fucking get over it. She's my old lady. He hasn't even seen her in years, he has no claim on her."

Viper gave a small nod and moved up a flight of stairs. The Satan's Cowboy's clubhouse was an old hotel. Three floors of various rooms. Wasn't a bad setup, especially for a club as big as theirs. Up on the third floor Viper slowed down.

"Our lock-up rooms are up the end here."

He pulled out a set of keys as he stopped in front of a prospect. "You can head off now. Job's done."

"Yes, prez."

The big guy lumbered away and Viper led us further down to a room with a barred door on it.

"Stone, you calmed the fuck down yet, brother?"

"Yeah, prez. You can let me out."

"Not until you promise me you won't go after Animal."

A growl filled the air. "You know he was rougher than he needed to be with her."

"Yeah, well, we don't call him Animal for the fucking fun of it. I'll let you get in the ring with him later, but you are not to go after him outside of that. We clear?"

"Yes, prez. Crystal, fucking clear."

"Good."

With that, Viper unlocked the door and took a step back. It was like looking at a ghost of my past when Stone walked out. Closely cropped hair, messy beard, and hard fucking eyes. He was bigger than he'd been back in the Middle East. Guess he'd spent his time since then bulking up.

"Stone."

"Taz." He came to stand right in front of me. "Don't like my sister being an old lady. She's a fucking accountant, and should be off somewhere married to a desk jockey and pumping out some grandkids for our folks."

"That just proves how little you know her. That life would drive her insane in a fucking heartbeat."

His glare intensified but I didn't back down. I took him down once before, I could do it again. He was bigger now, but then so was I. And when it came to Flick, I wasn't gonna let anything get in my way.

"Hurt her, I'll come after you."

Then before I could say a word in response, he shoved past me and left.

"Okay, then. That was nice and dramatic. Now, come get your girl and get out of here before something else fucking happens. I'm over the drama today."

I didn't need to be told twice. A second later I was rushing into the room. A lump formed in my throat at the sight of my Flick sitting there beaten to hell, but smiling up at me.

"Hear you had an interesting morning."

"Yeah, you could say that. How about you?"

I strode over to her and pulled her up off the bed and against me. Wrapping my arms around her, I palmed the back of her head to cradle it against my shoulder. Having her warm body pressed against mine finally allowed me to let go of my fear for her.

"Fuck, Flick. You've taken ten years off my life today."

She shuddered against me when I pressed a kiss to the top of her head, avoiding the wound on the back.

"Let's get home. You right to ride? Because Scout offered to tie you to me if you can't hang on."

That got a chuckle out of her. "I'm sure he did, but I can hang on. How far away are we?"

"We're up in Cutler, about a four hour ride home."

"Damn. That's one hell of a ride."

"We'll stop a few times. You'll be fine, but Scout wants to get back home tonight. We brought most of the club with us to come get you."

She rubbed her face against my shirt. "Really? Why?"

Cupping her face, I tilted it up so I could hold her gaze. "You're my old lady, my property. That makes you club property, we protect what's ours."

Her eyes filled with moisture but she blinked it away. "Is that why you asked me? To give me protection?"

I shook my head. "I asked you because I like fucking you on the regular."

Then, I kissed her before she could say something else. I didn't want her thinking so much about my reasons for making her mine. So long as she still wanted to be my old lady after everything that had happened today, things were good.

"C'mon, you two. We don't have time for you to have your reunion fuck here and now."

"Damn, Scout, you're such a giver."

"Yeah, well, with Taz you gotta be, or we'd be watching our very own live porn show for the next hour or so. Damn man has stamina, that's for sure."

Listening to Scout and Viper talk about me like I wasn't standing right here was pissing me off. "You two done?"

Scout grinned. "If you are."

With a shake of my head, I turned back to Flick. "You all right to walk or do you want me to carry you down?"

"I want to walk."

"No attacking anyone on your way out, you hear me?"

With a smirk, she nodded to Viper, then I took her hand and led her out of the room and down the hallway. If I wasn't so on edge over her injuries, I'd laugh at the way all the men tried their best to get out of our way while watching Flick with caution. In short order we were all back on our bikes, and with Flick's arms wrapped around me, we took off. For some reason, I was still on edge but I couldn't put my finger on why. The fact Scout had been fucking strange around Flick didn't help ease my thoughts.

No matter how late it was when we got home, I knew it wouldn't be the end of the day for us.

About Lexi Blake

Lexi Blake lives in North Texas with her husband, three kids, and the laziest rescue dog in the world. She began writing at a young age, concentrating on plays and journalism. It wasn't until she started writing romance that she found success. She likes to find humor in the strangest places. Lexi believes in happy endings no matter how odd the couple, threesome or foursome may seem. She also writes contemporary Western ménage as Sophie Oak.

Connect with Lexi online:

Facebook: Lexi Blake
Twitter: authorlexiblake
Website: www.LexiBlake.net